Clamor of Innocence

Central American Short Stories

Edited by
Barbara Paschke and David Volpendesta

City Lights Books
San Francisco

Front cover: "Night Language." Wool tapestry woven by Fernando Sánchez Sosa and Crispina López de Sánchez, from an oil painting by Elly Simmons.

Design: Patricia Fujii

Library of Congress Cataloging-in-Publication Data

Clamor of innocence : Central American short stories / edited by Barbara Paschke & David Volpendesta.

p. cm.

ISBN 0-87286-227-5

1. Short stories, Central American—Translations into English.
2. Short stories, English—Translations from Spanish. I. Paschke, Barbara.
II. Volpendesta, David.

PQ7087.E5C5 1988 88-16862

863'.01'08972—dc19 CIP

City Lights Books are available to bookstores through our primary distributor: Subterranean Company, P.O. Box 10233, Eugene, OR 97440. (503) 343-6324. Our books are also available through library jobbers and regional distributors. For personal orders and catalogs, please write to City Lights Books, 261 Columbus Avenue, San Francisco, CA 94133.

CITY LIGHTS BOOKS are edited by Lawrence Ferlinghetti and Nancy J. Peters and published at the City Lights Bookstore, 261 Columbus Avenue, San Francisco, CA 94133.

Dedicated to
our son Galen

NOTES ON WRITERS

JUAN ABURTO is a Nicaraguan who has published several books of short stories, among them *Narraciones* and *El Convivio.* MANLIO ARGUETA, a recipient of the *Casa de las Americas* prize, is a Salvadorean writer living in exile in Costa Rica. Two of his novels have been translated into English: *A Day of Life* and *Cuzcatlán.* ARTURO ARIAS is an exiled Guatemalan, living in Mexico. He has twice been awarded the *Casa de las Americas* prize. MIGUEL ANGEL ASTURIAS, the internationally renowned Guatemalan writer, received the Nobel Prize for Literature in 1967. EDUARDO BÄHR is a Honduran who has published two books of short stories *Fotografía del Peñasco* and *El Cuento de la Guerra.* ERNESTO CARDENAL is known worldwide as a poet and the Nicaraguan Minister of Culture. HORACIO CASTELLANOS MOYA was born in Honduras and grew up in El Salvador. He's the author of a novella, *La Travesía.* ROBERTO CASTILLO is a young Honduran whose two books of short stories are *Subida Al Cielo (y otros cuentos)* and *El Corneta.* LIZANDRO CHÁVEZ ALFARO received the *Casa de las Americas* prize for *Los Monos de San Telmo.* He has translated many North American writers, among them William Faulkner, into Spanish. DELFINA COLLADO is a Costa Rican writer. FABIÁN DOBLES, from Costa Rica, was awarded the *Premio Nacional de Literatura.* He is the author of short stories, and novels. JULIO ESCOTO is a Honduran writer of fiction. Two of his novels are *El Arbol de los Pañuelos* and *Días de Ventisca, Noches de Huracán.* DAVID ESCOBAR GALINDO is a Salvadorean. FRANCISCO GAVIDIA was born in El Salvador in 1863 and is one of the precursors of Central American Modernism. A master of the short story, he was also a dramatist and poet, who translated the French symbolists into Spanish. FERNANDO GORDILLO, a Nicaraguan poet and essayist, died in 1967. He was 26. ENRIQUE JARAMILLO LEVI is a Panamanian dramatist, short story writer, and poet. He's currently at the University of Texas on a Fullbright Scholarship. DANTE LIANO is an exiled Guatemalan, living in Mexico. HUGO LINDO, a Salvadorean poet who died recently, has two poetry books translated into English, *Only the Voice* and *Facile Word.* CARMEN LYRA was born in Costa Rica in 1888 and died while exiled in Mexico in 1949. Her most famous book is *Los Cuentos de Mi Tía Panchita.* ALVARO MENDENDEZ FRANCO is a Panamanian writer. AUGUSTO MONTERROSO, a Guatemalan, is an essayist and translator. His most important books are *Obras Completas y otros cuentos* and *La Oveja Negra y Demás Fábulas.* MARIO ROBERTO MORALES is an exiled Guatemalan writer living in Costa Rica. He received the 1985 EDUCA Prize for his novel *El Esplendor del Pirámide.* CARMEN NARANJO, a Costa Rican novelist and poet, is the editor of EDUCA. Among her many published books are, *Diario de Una Multitud* (a novel) and *Mi Guerrilla,* an epic poem. JORGE LUIS OVIEDO is a Honduran poet, who has written short fiction, collected in *La Muerte Más Aplaudida* and *Cincocuentos.* BERTALICIA PERALTA is a Panamanian poet and journalist. Among her books are *Barcarola y Otras Fantasías Incorregibles* and *Muerto en Enero.* SERGIO RAMÍREZ is the Vice-President of Nicaragua and an internationally-known fiction writer whose works have been translated into many languages. BESSY REYNA is a Panamanian writer and critic who lives in Connecticut, where she edits the bilingual magazine *El Taller Literario.* SAMUEL ROVINSKI is a Costa Rican essayist, novelist, and playwright. Among his many published works are *Ceremonia de Casta* (a novel) and *Un Modelo para Rosaura* (a play). SALARRUÉ (Salvador Salazar Arrué), the late Salvadorean writer and painter, is one of Central America's most highly respected writers. His selected works have been published by the University of El Salvador. ROGELIO SINÁN is a Panamanian writer, professor, and diplomat. Among his books are *Dos Aventuras en el Lejano Oriente* and *Semana Santa en la Niebla.* RIMA VALLBONA is a Costa Rican writer residing in Houston, Texas. *Noche en Vela* and *Polvo del Camino* are two of her several books of fiction.

NOTES ON TRANSLATORS

TINA ALVAREZ ROBLES contributed translations to *Volcán* and *Tomorrow Triumphant.* Recently, she translated Mario Roberto Morales' novel, *El Esplendor del Pirámide* into English. DAN BELLM is a San Francisco translator and freelance journalist who has written widely on Latin America. LELAND CHAMBERS is a Professor of English and Comparative Literature at the University of Denver, and translator of Ezequiel Martínez Estrada. THOMAS CHRISTENSEN, a former editor at North Point Press, translated Julio Cortazar's *Around the Day in Eighty Worlds* and is now translating a book of short stories by Carlos Fuentes. ELIZABETH GAMBLE MILLER is an Associate Professor of Foreign Languages and Literature at Southern Methodist University. She translated Hugo Lindo's books of poems into English. STEVE HELLMAN is a San Francisco writer, translator, and freelance journalist. SEAN HIGGINS is an Oakland-based translator. ALBERTO HUERTA, S.J. a poet, essayist, and translator, is an Assistant Professor of Romance Languages at the University of San Francisco. STEPHEN KESSLER has translated books by Nobel Prize-winning poet Vincente Aleixander and exiled Chilean poet Fernando Alegría. SYLVIA MULLALLY AGUIRRE is a KPFA radio host, and a journalist who writes for the weekly Spanish language newspaper *El Mensajero.* BARBARA PASCHKE co-edited Volcán, Roque Dalton's *Poemas Clandestinos,* and has contributed translations to many other anthologies and journals. DAVID VOLPENDESTA is a poet and freelance journalist who has written extensively on Latin American culture and politics. He also co-edited Otto René Castillo's selected poems, *Tomorrow Triumphant* and *Homeless not Helpless.* KATHLEEN WEAVER translated Omar Cabezas's best selling *Testimonio, Fire From the Mountain,* and is currently translating Julio Cortazar's *Nicaragua Tan Violentomente Dulce.*

Leland Chambers, Thomas Christensen, Stephen Kessler, Elizabeth Gamble Miller, Barbara Paschke, and Kathleen Weaver are members of ALTA, The American Literary Translators Association.

Acknowledgements: A special thanks to Carmen Naranjo, Christian Santos, Yolanda Ingianna, Claribel Alegría, Mario Roberto Morales, Manlio Argueta, Bud Flakoll, EDUCA, Sherman Carroll of Readers International, and Meighan Pritchard, Patricia Fujii, Nancy J. Peters, Robert Sharrard, and Lawrence Ferlinghetti of City Lights.

Some of these short stories have appeared in the following magazines and books: The Fever Heroes, *El Nuevo Cuento Hondureño.* © Dardo Editores. Walls, *Ondina.* © EDUCA. The Grey Phantom, *Cuentos Judíos de Mi Tierra.* © Editorial Costa Rica. A Train Ride, *Aquí Se Cuentan Cuentos.* © Hugo Lindo. Penelope on Her Silver Wedding Anniversary, *Mujeres y Agonías.* © Arte Público Press. An Antistory, *Cuentos y Anticuentos.* © Editorial Universitaria Panamá. Highnoon in April, *La Balada del Herido Pájaro (y otros relatos).* © Servicios Editoriales Centroamericanos. Heaven's Surgeon, *Cuentos de Rogelio Sinán.* © EDUCA. Clamor of Innocence, *Trece Veces Nunca.* © Editorial Nueva Nicaragua. Katok, *Tierra Oscura.* © EDUCA. We Bad, *Cuentos de Barro.* ©EDUCA. The Guayacan Tree, © Bertalicia Peralta. A Surrender of Love, *Prosa Narrativa.* © Ediciones Primavera Popular 5. The Last Flight of the Sly Bird, *Cincocuentos.* © Dardo Editores. Democrash, ©Dante Liano. The Clean Ashtrays, *Ab Ovo.* © Ediciones Instituto Nacional de Cultura. Orders, *El Cuento Nicaraguense.* © Ediciones El Pez y La Serpiente. The She-wolf, *Cuentos y Narraciones.* © EDUCA. The Woman in the Middle, ©Arturo Arias. Johnthe, *Antología del Cuento Centroamericano.* © EDUCA. The Swede, *Antología del Cuento Centroamericano.* © EDUCA. The Barricade, *La Rebelión de las Imágenes, Relatos (1962-72).* © Editorial "Nosotros." Deadweight, © Mario Roberto Morales. Setback, *Perfil de Prófugo.* © Claves Latinoamericanas. Estefanía, *Antología del Cuento Centroamericano.* © EDUCA. Taking Over the Streets, © Manlio Argueta. The Centerfielder, *Antología del Cuento Centroamericano.* © EDUCA and English translation by special arrangement with Readers International. The Bridge, *Cuentos Escogidos.* © Editorial Educativa Costarricense. While He Lay Sleeping, *Duplicaciones.* © Joaquin Mortiz. Anita, the Insect Hunter, *Subida Al Cielo (y otros cuentos).* © Extension Universitaria. Mr. Taylor, *Antología del Cuento Centroamericano.* ©EDUCA. In translation; The Grey Phantom appeared in *Response: A Contemporary Jewish Review.* Spring 87. We Bad appeared in *Zyzzyva,* Summer 88.

TABLE OF CONTENTS

THE FEVER HEROES

Eduardo Bähr

Translated by Thomas Christensen

Papa:

I am sending this letter with Sr. Morales or Norales, who says he is an advance guard for the Red Cross. Here nobody knows who is who. Not since huge numbers of freshly armed and uniformed civilians have arrived. They've put up a cross on several large tents that seem to be intended for hospitals. And all the trucks coming in carry vast stores of food and medicine.

My colonel is like an old lady—why are they making all this fuss and why don't they go where the real action is, he says, and he even threatened to drag them off himself. We've received orders to keep close to these bombed villages because they think infantry will be coming, but we have plenty of time and not a soul has shown up yet. For the moment all we do is clean our weapons and shine our boots. With the arrival of these civilians the business looks for all the world like a village fair. Everybody is bustling around, and while some old women, who seem to be part of the outfit, are making mountains of food that they're going to eat themselves, there are others who sing and sound like they really dip into the bottle. A little while ago one of these fellows asked me if I was one of the enemy or one of us. I couldn't help myself, I told him to fuck off before I let him have it, and he went away saying I was a crude and vulgar ass.

Among those arriving in the trucks are some characters who say they're going to put on a show, or something like that. They're setting up a stage and painting their faces. There are some young women with whorish faces that even God could not disguise who came with them and who have dedicated themselves to visiting the officers' tents. So as we wait for the enemy we're well off in this respect, and although some of my companions are hoping to be transferred to the line of fire, I'm not, because I don't know what I'll do the first time I fire a shot into the body of another man like myself.

I must say I don't have many friends here. I hardly speak to anyone because I feel out of place in this uniform, carrying this ton of ammunition. I've told you I don't like this war business, and I guess you must have told Leonel to keep an eye on me.

He keeps hanging around; he gives me busywork to do when I'm idle; he makes me do watch duty where they think the enemy will appear, and all the time he makes fun of me. Yesterday when we settled in he told me not to think that just because I'm his brother he's going to treat me with kid gloves. I just hope this whole business is over soon and I can get out of here. Tell Mama I'm well and I hope to see her soon. And don't let Celina touch the books I left behind. To you I send a big hug.

Your son who loves you,
Hernan

P.S. Tell Celina to water the avocado tree I grafted and to remember to feed Hurricane and that I'll bring her a surprise from the border.

Papa:

I don't know if you'll get this letter. I'm writing it in a rare moment of rest. Excuse the paper and my handwriting. We're engaged in action near the border, I can't tell you exactly where because the supply master, who says he will deliver this, assures me it's forbidden. I can tell you we've come upon several villages that the enemy has already been through. The people come out with their pigs and potbellied kids, who are practically naked, all of them. This war business is even more screwed up than I thought. And I have to tell you that when we came upon one woman who asked where we were from, we jumped her without answering. I didn't, but all my companions did. Then we rushed off in an advance and the men I was with left me and I lost my gear; then I came upon some dead soldiers and they were from the other side so I took a couple of guns from them and headed for the mountains. I soon arrived, tired and very much afraid, and Leonel told everybody I had killed some enemy soldiers. But I hadn't killed anyone, and don't think me a coward but ever since the fighting began I've had to close my eyes and fire blindly and (I can tell this to you) I've never liked the idea of killing anyone—but if Leonel knew that he would be capable of killing me. So far we've only fired at a distance; we just see their powder flashes and hear some enormous howitzers that I think are 105s. In the morning we found piles of dead men and they were the ones who go in advance with machetes and behead the lookouts—Intibucas, who are like animals with this weapon. We've also been joined by some Indians from Mount Flores, who never speak and go around half dressed, and—get this—their only weapons are long, thin spears that are supposed to be poisoned. The villages stink to high heaven and they've all been plundered. We've even come across women's underwear strung up between poles so we'd see them, in the abandoned church too, and they've left the mark of the Devil's Brigade and others that seem to be those of a certain Medrano, and the signs say they'll be back. Last night we ran into some soldiers who called out Come on, we're Hondurans, but the captain said Nobody move, and we didn't say anything. It made me remember how we had come across some members of the Special Security Corps on the highway and Leonel told them to identify themselves and they just shot back, and Leonel ordered fire and five of them were killed and they were from our side. But this time it was the captain who spoke and asked what was the name of their batallion, and they didn't answer, they just said they were on our side. So we were there for about half an hour facing each other without saying a word, with our arms drawn, some five meters apart in the darkness, until finally they moved and went away without saying anything. I was touching my crucifix the whole time but the captain didn't see me.

That's all for now because we're about to move; I'll just mention that we're about to be transferred to the other front because the tactics division is on its way here. Maybe when we arrive at Nacaome I'll send you another letter; for now just give my regards to Mama, tell her I'm well by God's will, and give my regards too to Hurricane and Celina. To you a hug from your son who loves you.

Hernan

Papa:

Last night I was wounded but don't worry it isn't serious. Tell Mama not to worry either. They grabbed me when I was on watch in a *guama* tree and you can bet I was grabbed by a horrible fear; if I hadn't jumped I think they would have killed me. The others kidded me that I yelled like Tarzan and began to fire away like a madman. I have a little fever but the bad thing is there's nothing to eat. This afternoon we were going to look for chickens to steal but we didn't find any because the people had all fled. There are some green brambleberries and *vaca gorda* leaves, so we won't die of starvation and thirst since now no one sends us anything from Tegucigalpa, which is probably already in the hands of the enemy. You can hide in Uncle Julian and Aunt Maria Andino's house, which is well hidden on the mountain. That's if you receive this letter. Leonel is going to what is supposed to be a big battle for some highways in a place called El Ujuste, and it must be big because they've been fighting for something like six hours and they pile up the wounded and it's enough to make your hair stand on end because they let out these screams, and since I'm among them I see they may have been hit by grenades and half their chest is a mass of wet blood and shreds of uniform or their heads are in pieces and they howl and choke with their dying gasps. They make me want to stay on the highway and see if I can make it home but I'm waiting for Leonel to tell him what I'm going to do and if he wants to kill me to just go ahead. Don't worry, just a joke.

The people here say that the enemy must have reached Puerto Cortés via Santa Rosa because there was no one from the Fourth Zone there; we had expected them to be in the defensive region of Colomoncagua, and specifically the area of Merendón, but no one has reached us to explain. They also say that they're fighting in El Ticante and that the O.A.S. is going to work out something to put a halt to the killing. Some of them came through here and they told the colonel that the enemy now isn't bombing with heavy arms, but the colonel said we're opening enough holes ourselves to sow a coffee plantation, and when they left their helicopter was shot at.

I can't tell you when all this might end, but it looks bad. My fever is increasing a little, but it's nothing, don't worry. You can tell Celina she can read my books if she wants, they're a gift, and you can sell Hurricane, who is supposed to be purebred and might bring in some money to help you move away from there. Tell Celina not to worry about the avocado tree I was taking care of because I'm going to sow a forest here before this affair is over, there's plenty of fertilizer with all the bones lying around. Just a little joke.

Take care, Papa, you know I love you and I don't want to worry you with all my problems. If anyone says anything to you about your place of birth, tell them you're as Honduran as the next, and you even have two brave sons in battle. And you know, they're even calling one of them the hero of the Pedregal, which is me.

And now I'm going to say goodbye because I'm very tired and the others never stop wailing, but it's nothing for you to worry about.

Your son.

"You remember, Papa, how you used to give me a hard time about spending my time swimming in the river with my schoolmates. You remember how you told me I'd never be good for anything and you told me to follow the example of Leonel, who was studying to be a military cadet, whereas I was nothing. You remember, Papa, when we were on that tin roof during the flood and you didn't speak for two days and I swam in the water with Celina while the swollen cows and people in canoes went by until a helicopter came and you told the gringo the children hadn't eaten, meaning us. You remember, hmm? Because I'm remembering all these things now like they're happening to me and they're coming at me one after another like a whistling locomotive, I hear its piercing sound, I'm in the middle of the noises and surrounded by the black smoke, chuggachugga, in the second-class cars they want to buy bread, the bread goes by, it's forbidden to go into the first-class cars, Papa, you're tired of knocking yourself out to support us, where is my mother, not the mother of Leonel whom I call mother but my real mother, you never talk to me about her, Papa, look at this putrid water with its filthy froth and the rescuers fastening a knot on that one's leg, there are bursting cows, and Papa, what do you think, things are not so hard here, look at the people going by with their guts in their hands and an old man like you, Papa, who goes along holding back the blood running from his eyes and my friends here whose names I don't even know in that damp earth, dancing heads down and hands flailing, dancing, dancing to the sergeant's command, the dance of death, I dance, you dance, he dances, we are alive, and this gun is heavy, Papa, like when you told me you followed Ferrera, I'm the hero now, the hero of the Pedregal, Papa, I go around pulling the wounded from their holes, the holes where the dead lie with their blank eyes, I pull them out while the bullets sing around me, and the sergeant tells me don't be a fool and I fire my rifle in order to pull out another poor soul, not to kill, Papa, in school I cried when I killed a snake, a little snake that crawled away thinking it could escape, Iris was watching me and I nailed it with a heel and the blood came to my ears and she ran away crying and the pretty snake kept coming at me, its severed neck wagging its head, sticking out its bloody tongue, the hero of the Pedregal, when the grenade fell I closed my eyes and on one side they were firing and I grabbed them with my heart in my hands and they say I saved them, so many years, Papa, you were in the company, so many years, tired yardworker, all day, the sun, you with your machine rroarring and pushing, how you sweat, Papa, you sweat, the sun, such heat, I'm drowning in your sweat, it fills my eyes, and those who are screeching here like decapitated hogs, they are, you're right, give me the bucket, blood of pigs, don't look at me, Papa, I'm turning cold and pale, my hands are trembling and the pail is filling up with blood in the slaughterhouse, the same as the slaughterhouse, you see blood and you hear the oxen squeal, Papa, the sweaty arm with the sledgehammer that slams the forehead and splits the head, the sound of bones, Papa, go, they are looking for Salvadorans, they'll throw you in the river, defend yourself, fire a shot like this one, Papa, if you are my father, what heat chokes my neck they are bayonetting me, and since I can't move let me go I'm not going to kill anyone, Papa, my chest hurts, you can see, this whole side is full of lead, and they stuck the bayonet in me here, how can I bear this pain if I am a man, don't you know, I close my eyes when I fire and if I kill and faint in front of my brother, dear brother, don't make fun of me, don't put me where they'll kill me, that's not for me, can't you see, brother, that I'm not a man like you, that you fight and kill for your country, me too with my eyes shut ten clowns covering their pieces in the air, I shoot, see how they fall, destroyed, I don't hear the shot, the noise opens the mouth blood runs out, it runs out the back as if I had dropped a tree on them I turn around green sound of broken bones, such heat they are swallowing, Papa, it hurts to cry when you drink, Papa, I'm drowning in this salty sweat, nobody is coming and I'm drowning, they don't come, take out this knife, I'm going with Lizandro Vega, satiate all these dead assholes, these dead children, these earthen colors that are rotting there, let's go, old Lizandro Vega, on the river of the flood, the burning river, now you see I am macho, I'm going to stop drifting and drinking, don't get mad, don't hit me, I don't know what I want to be but I don't want you to send me to the line, my dear little father, Mama, tell him not to send me, I won't go with Leonel, don't make me, dear little mother, I'm drowning in this river of heat, shut their traps stop the screaming don't cry like that, please, dear God, what shit I'm doing here pulling out this drowned corpse, by the foot, pulling this rope and this cursed one is stiff, I can't pull him out, the current, if I let him go Papa will be angry, save me someone, I am drowning in this foul water, salty, water, pull me out, I can myself, I am a man, pull me out, pull me, Papa, but now let's go, don Lizandro, let's go..."

WALLS

Carmen Naranjo

Translated by Barbara Paschke

I wonder why I was given this assignment? A response is a response, he says to himself as he watches the flight of a dark bird against the background of the clear blue sky, as they say in national anthems.

The meeting's to be here. He found it a natural place. A little town on hills of eucalyptus and pine, spread out to where the plains begin, with five blocks crowded with houses and the rest scattered among the streams and the lazy river bordered by stones and huge rocks where ferns grew and where lizards lay almost immobile.

In the hotel, a large old house with hallways all going toward the cobbled patio in the center full of tangled vines with meaty leaves and reddish flowers, they ask him how many days he's planning to stay. He says three. "Are you sure?" "Very sure, because I have other plans."

The room is dark and he finds it narrow and oppressive, the walls humid and spotted with mushrooms, which appear to be moving around on a badly drawn map. He leaves his small suitcase and goes out to look for the plaza and the church.

Bells are tolling for a funeral. Would this make it difficult to find the man? Fifth row on the side aisle, counting from the pulpit. White shirt, gray pants, and a black hat on his knees.

Old women in mourning are hurrying toward the plaza. A package tomorrow. Another on Tuesday in front of the altar. The last on Wednesday near the Chapel of the Poor Souls. Some children holding flowers are waiting at the corner. A family, all in black, crosses the street.

The Church is neglected but beautiful, with thick columns on which vines and grape branches climb and which on one side have images of the Holy Family, St. Joseph, the Virgin Mary, Baby Jesus, and on the other side, a fat and smiling saint, completely unknown but obviously the town's patron.

The bells toll, lacking the seriousness of the occasion, having instead a cheerful ring. Or else the bell ringer doesn't know what he's doing or suffers in happiness for other people's sorrow.

Over on a hill a tall pine is going up in flames, collapsing with crackling and hissing and frightening the neighbors. Perhaps it was struck by unexpected lightning.

When he goes up the stairway, a dead bird falls near his feet. Perhaps it died in flight.

In the vestibule near the door, one of the beggars shows him a bloody empty hole that looks as though he had just pulled out his eye.

The church smells of incense and freshly cut lilies. It's full. From the back he counts the pews and in the fifth one there are six men wearing white shirts.

He waits while he listens to the lapidary requiem for the pine coffin. At the end four men carry it off. Solemn faces, carved in sadness. Further back a group walking arm in arm weep with their faces hidden. The funeral procession is a mix of peasants and workers.

When he sees the empty pew, the fifth, he sinks down in the middle of it and waits. He hears footsteps behind him and waits for the tap on his shoulder. He remembers the password. During the night the walls walk.

An hour goes by. Nothing, no one. Another hour goes by. Nothing, no one, not even a devout old woman. Another hour. Better to come back tomorrow.

Lonely streets that seem even narrower lead him back to the hotel, and a lonely hallway takes him to his room. There he's surprised by how narrow it is. It looks like a cell. Moreover, he remembers that he left his suitcase in the middle of the room and now it's up against the wall, which, under careful inspection, looks as if it's become even blacker with mushrooms and feels as if it's grown thicker.

He sleeps badly because he thinks he feels the walls closing in and the mushrooms growing. It's hot in the room. It occurs to him to note the distance between the walls: eight feet wide by twelve feet long. More than a room, it's a niche, he says to himself, while he notices there are other spots of mushrooms, and maybe there's no mystery—maybe it's just that the paint is peeling because of the heat and the humidity. Several times he steps out the door in search of some open space to find out if it's dawn; his watch stopped when he arrived in town. But dawn is still a long way off, and each time he looks the darkness deepens. A heavy sleep envelops him in the early morning, and noon catches him in bed sweating, with bad breath. "Damn! I missed the nine o'clock appointment this morning and if he's not there at four, I'm taking the first flight out tomorrow."

At exactly four o'clock, passing through streets that are now really alleys, he finds the church empty, and empty he leaves it at seven, when the sacristan tells him he has to close up. What's going on, he wonders, maybe he didn't get the package, but he could have let me know, losing time like this and going back with nothing; the clients are really going to raise a stink.

In the hotel he's told that there won't be a plane until the airport is repaired; his flight was the last to land. And by road? Yes, that will be possible when the washed-out bridge is rebuilt. This can't be happening.

He walks through streets that seem like hallways. What am I going to do? Return to that room? Never! The night's getting cold. Returning to the hotel, he asks if there isn't another room; his is too small. They're all the same, sir, and they're all occupied.

The room seems even smaller and the walls are almost completely black with mushrooms. He measures seven feet wide by twelve feet long. It could be that during the night, half asleep, he didn't count correctly. Besides, he has to figure out how to get out, how the hell to get out of this damned town.

He puts his suitcase in order, without knowing why. He tries to remember and remembers only yesterday's funeral, the sound of the bells, the pine tree writhing amidst the flames, the dead bird falling at his feet, the beggar's bloody empty eye socket, the men's faces, the coffin, the procession. Yesterday's corpse, could that have been who he's waiting for?

Luck had always accompanied him. Always. In the worst times, when everything was against him, luck was there, on his side, saving him time and again. It wasn't fair to think it had left him now; that would be challenging luck. But they say luck gives out, changes, and things become different. He whistles and looks for a deck of cards to play a game of solitaire on the bed. If he wins, luck is with him, and if he loses, well, it's gone. The room shakes, yes, shakes. Violently! He opens the door and runs. In the hallway, no one, in the alley, no one. Those alleys, more and more shrunken, labyrinthine, almost mere passageways. A dead bird falls between his feet.

He returns to his room, and as he goes through the door he senses that the walls have moved. He counts again: five feet wide by ten feet long. It seems like a nightmare. It could have been the tremor. The best thing would be for the sun to come up soon. He gathers up the cards, feels it's better not to challenge luck. He tries to sleep and forget.

He hears a storm approaching; the distant thunder comes closer and a torrent of water falls on the roof. The roar inundates the room. It rains hard. The storm moves further away. It's time to rest, and the lullaby of the rain brings sleep. He moves the bed to get it away from the walls so he'll be able to know if this rare phenomenon is real, that here the walls walk, as the password says. Really, what a strange coincidence! Everything in this town is strange, even its name, Walls. Sleep closes his eyes as he debates with himself about staying awake, because strange things happen here, and sleeping, because the road will be long; he had planned to walk to the nearest town and there look for a way to get to the capital.

Around midnight, perhaps (time is so imprecise when one's watch doesn't work and the only reference point is darkness with no window), he wakes up, startled. Using his hands he confirms that there's no distance between his bed and the walls, both at the sides of the mattress, and at the ends of the bed. He looks for the door and doesn't find it; he's locked in, he's in prison. Yes, the kind of punishment he deserves has now been discovered and he knows it. It's all been a trap. The message to come to Walls, the transfer of the package, the hotel, the last plane flight, the destroyed bridge, the rain of dead birds, the funeral. What a subtle form of entrapment! Too subtle for him, an ordinary anonymous dealer. Why so elaborate and so complicated? Without a doubt, it would have been easier to detain him, interrogate him, and put him in some prison, just as he deserved. He did things with care, but there are always loose ends which only luck succeeds in tying up in favor of innocence, his innocence of appearing to be an anonymous being, a peaceful good citizen, an insignificant person no one pays any attention to. But underneath, an undesirable, and no one likes undesirables; they always want to capture them, torture them, and leave them to rot as they deserve.

The bed cracks, the walls are advancing. Another tremor, strong. The tremor hurls him down on the bed, which collapses on the floor.

A piece of plaster, hostile and sharp, falls on top of him. The end of the world. Yes, the end of the world, just as his grandmother said it would happen, December 31 at twelve midnight.

And the walls come together over the consciousness of someone who has been abandoned by luck for the first time.

He was found several days later. By then, swollen and foul smelling, his eyes open in terror. Indolence and bad service prevailed in the hotel. The cashier said the guy in room 21 had already been there a week and he figured he'd probably run out because there were no signs of life. There on top of the bed, half naked, he completely lost all sense of time and obligation to pay his debts. Later, the police searched thoroughly and found nothing to confirm the name and information he gave when he registered at the hotel. They called the number he'd given as his home phone, but a laundry answered and didn't know him. The town nurse, the only one who, along with the pharmacist, officially gave vaccinations and prescribed medicine, said it was a heart attack, judging from the terror on his face, as if something sudden and unexpected had come over him.

With nothing to do, no one to notify, they buried him in a corner of some public land, with no more formality than wrapping him in a sheet and putting him in a box that was inexpensive because the lid was made of a different wood and didn't fit very well.

The beggar with the bloody empty socket, master of all the dead birds, said to the other beggar, "Have you noticed that death is carrying away all the visitors to Walls?" "Really," answered the other, "I wonder why...?"

THE GREY PHANTOM

Samuel Rovinski

Translated by Dan Bellm

It was the first time Herman had gotten up from his cot with an urge to get to work. For once the bright rays of sun, slipping in through scraps of blanket nailed up against the dirty window screen, didn't bother him.

On other mornings, when the intense light hurt his eyes and made him see fire in his dreams, he would work his head under the pillow and press it against himself until it hurt. Then the nightmare would disappear in a flash of color, and the music of a military band would creep into his ears. In the haze, a few musicians, more like skeletons with parchment for skin than human beings, would be scraping rusty, cobwebbed violins and blaring horns and trumpets. The melody would be out of tune but vigorous, ordering him into an endless line of men, women, and children. Their naked bodies showed marks of brutal torture, and they dragged themselves resignedly, step by step, while grey-uniformed soldiers observed them with a scornful hatred. The music would force him to march to his assigned position—number 135878, which they had tattooed on his right arm—and to endure the soldiers' humiliations until they ended over there, in the awful place from which no one returns, with no right of clemency even to plead for his life, because the men in grey uniforms had crushed his will and his defiant rage.

The deceitful music tells him he must obey, fall into line and keep moving forward. But Herman shrinks from the order, stops up his ears, closes his eyes, and tosses desperately on the cot. Furiously he struggles to escape from the men in grey. One of them is trying to push him into a dark, ominous tunnel. He strikes out, bites, yells, and his cry multiplies in the emptiness. He doesn't stop yelling, because he knows that at the end of the long line of emaciated bodies, flames wait to devour him until his charred bones are dumped in the ditch full of the bones of those who came before him—the ditch the victims dug themselves.

Now when he opens his eyes there are no more soldiers or corpses and the music has vanished; there is only the clear light of day.

Herman sat on the edge of the cot to stretch himself awake. With a tug he set aside the wool blanket stained with oil and bits of onion from the pickled herring he'd smuggled out of the party at the Centro Israelita. He scratched his chest awhile. Although his wool nightshirt was buttoned up to the neck, the hairs of his apelike chest broke through and he began to play with them, trying to make himself ticklish.

When he stood up to put on his shirt, which hung from a nail on the termite-eaten plank wall, Herman hit his head against the light bulb, which began to spin, filling the room with strange morning shadows. Then he remembered that he hadn't turned the light off when he went to bed.

He whistled a tune but couldn't finish it. He whistled again and failed. The melody reminded him of something. He made another attempt and the sounds harmonized, then scattered. In his dim memory Herman sensed the message that always left him puzzled; it was like a chorus of voices singing his name in unison, warning him in a solemn tone about something he couldn't quite understand. He pricked up his ears, but in vain; the melody had vanished. So he stopped whistling.

He dressed quickly, locked the double armoire which tipped over with a groan at the foot of his cot, washed his face in the tiny basin in the corner, and walked to the bathroom down at the end of the hall.

Sitting on the pot he remembered the wedding feast and the food from last night. A satisfied look crossed his face as the banquet table of herring and pâté and dill pickles and chicken soup and tongue and other dishes passed by in review. Someone knocked insistently on the door and Herman had no choice but to leave.

On the sidewalk outside his miserable boardinghouse, he found that the city was already awake.

He walked down Calle 12 among early-morning prostitutes, tinkers opening their shops, shoemakers, and one or two drunks sprawled out on the sidewalk. He turned down Avenida 1, where a crowd of women was bustling over to the shop stalls of the Mercado Borbón, jostling among *campesinos* unloading fruits and vegetables.

The movement of people through the narrow sidewalks made him dizzy.

He climbed the hill with effort, observing with great interest the gesticulations and cries of the greengrocers, the women with their sacks and shopping bags, the bare-chested workers who carried sacks of flour or boxes of greens and vegetables or huge slabs of meat on shoulders barely protected with bits of rag.

Herman moved among the crowd like an elephant caught in a thicket. Without realizing it, he kept bumping into people who reacted first with indignation and then with fear. His gaze was piercing through the passers-by and the facades of buildings to settle in some gloomy, nebulous region of his stunted memory. Back there among jumbled recollections he saw a blurred line of houses coming toward him, which gave him a strange, uneasy feeling. He wanted either to cry or to shake with fear.

Finally he arrived at the shop. He stopped next to two workmen in front of the door, waiting for it to open. One of the men laughed at him, but Herman took it as a friendly gesture and returned a smile.

The shop owner arrived, accompanied by three men Herman recognized as board members of the Centro Israelita. They passed him without a greeting, but Don Luis said good moring and Herman hurried forward to help him lift the heavy door-latch.

Don Luis and the three board members went into the back room and sat down around a desk. After talking awhile they gave Herman the signal to come in.

Herman could see that they were discussing something in Yiddish. Don Luis was waving a newspaper and talking in a loud voice, red in the face and sweating. Herman couldn't understand what was making them so upset. From time to time he picked up words like anti-Semite,

Nazi, dangerous, Ulate, demonstration.... The blood froze in his veins when he heard the word "Nazi." It made him think of some horrible, imminent disaster, and he started to tremble.

After talking for quite a while the men reached an agreement and Don Luis took Herman aside to give him instructions.

Whistling contentedly, Herman stepped into the street. He had a mission that made him feel transformed, something completely different from his daily work routine. He hated passing out fliers for the board of directors or invitations for weddings and bar mitzvahs. He didn't like the way people treated him. If it weren't for his tips he would have told them all off a long time ago. No one talked to him except to give him orders. Children even ran away from him, or else made faces and mocked his appearance.

But this time they had entrusted him with a mission, him alone; they had let him know he was important, and so he felt proud, distinguished, conscious of a duty to fulfill. What's more, he had the whole morning and afternoon to spend as he pleased. Don Luis had given him the day off.

Sitting on a bench across from the atrium of the cathedral, Herman breathed deeply under the shade of a palm tree that had been spared the axe. He rolled up his trousers, exposing the varicose veins in his legs, then quickly took off his shoes to rub his tired feet. He stared at the pompous little newsstand shaped like a temple, and the mosaic footpaths that had displaced the fig trees, palms, and cypresses of an earlier time. Then he became engrossed in reviewing the instructions he had received.

A gang of shoeshine boys came along to taunt him with name-calling and crude gestures. Herman paid them no attention, busy as he was in refreshing his memory, but when one of the little brats threw a mango pit in his face, he suddenly was filled with an uncontrollable rage and jumped off his bench like a giant ape. Then the boys scattered down the paths in different directions, laughing and yelling, leaving Herman standing there shaking his fist in the air. Once he felt free of their harassment, his rage vanished and he felt like walking.

He crossed the park over to La Perla and sat down in a corner at the back. The waiter recognized him and brought over half a loaf of bread with butter and coffee with milk. Nearby two people were discussing soccer, a sunken-eyed, overnight drunk was nursing his bit of rum, another was buried in his newspaper, and a boy was shining a well-dressed fellow's shoes. The atmosphere fascinated Herman; the human warmth and bustle of the café made him feel alive.

When he was halfway through his coffee, Herman heard an unusual commotion out in the street. He swallowed down the rest, paid the bill, and went over to look out one of the doorways of La Perla.

An aggressive crowd of people was starting to gather at the entrance of the *Diario de Costa Rica,* waving signs with slogans such as "Business is for Costa Ricans," "Undesirable foreigners get out!" and "Go plant potatoes, Polacks!"

Herman scratched his head; he couldn't understand these people. Why were they telling the Polish to go plant potatoes? His memory hardly reached into his past life, but he was sure of one thing—he had never planted potatoes before. The picket signs and the menacing cries of these people in the street made him remember something.

In his tattered memory he seemed to see people breaking windows and beating old men and women in streets lined with buildings taller than these. It was a different city, where people spoke a different language, but the threats were much the same. Suddenly he could hear the stamping feet of soldiers, the cocking of rifles and machine guns, orders cried out—but the vision vanished. The same people were in the street, and not a single soldier.

On the second-floor wall of the *Diario de Costa Rica,* a man was scrawling the same slogans that the picket signs carried. The people down in the street were applauding and calling out "Viva Ulate!" and "Death to the Polacks!" It seemed to Herman that these people had gone mad, and he headed away from them down the Avenida Central. The avenue was almost deserted, with almost all the shops closed up and a number of policemen standing guard in the Plaza de la Artilleria.

For the rest of the day Herman wandered around the city, and when the sun went down he passed by the shop to pick up the synagogue keys and a bag of food for dinner.

Then he headed for the synagogue, a rambling old wooden house.

It was a clear night but the *barrio* was dark, dimly lit by an old streetlamp and the lights from the windows of neighboring houses.

Herman felt afraid to be out walking alone.

Down the next block a couple was nonchalantly making love in the doorway of the Canada Dry building. A dog wandered over to sniff at Herman's bag, only to end up with a kick that sent him off howling in pain. A warm breeze was dragging loose papers around the street, and a *ranchero* melody drifted out of the nearest cantina.

Herman passed the doorway and rushed the remaining distance

to the synagogue door, hurrying to open the padlock.

The sanctuary was dark as a tomb. Herman stopped, paralyzed with fear: had enemies come inside, waiting somewhere in the dark to kill him? But he couldn't hear a single sound or movement; the air was simply filled with the fragrance of old wood. Gradually he became used to the darkness and could see the benches, the wooden screen that marked off the women's area for prayer, and at the back, the Ark and the service leader's podium. He took courage and walked over to the nearest bench to sit down, setting his bag beside him. Soon he was devouring his dinner.

With a full stomach he felt more at home. His fear had vanished and now he looked calmly around the temple.

How lovely it would be for Herman to occupy this bench during prayers, when the room was full of people! But to sit here you needed to have money, you had to pay the membership dues and be respectable—he would have to resign himself to standing up at the back with his yellowed *talit* and his worn-out prayer book. Yet sitting here now, lord and master of the temple, and with an important mission besides, he felt he had not always been a nobody. Once he too had been decently dressed, clean, and well respected.

Suddenly Herman felt transported years back to the interior of a large temple, where a beautiful woman was smiling at him across the screen and a boy sitting next to him took his hand as he turned the pages of the prayer book. The vision struck him forcefully and the memory of the little boy gripped his heart. It was his son! Now he saw him quite clearly. The rabbi and his assistants were carrying the Torah scrolls up and down the aisles of the synagogue and the men were touching them gently with their phylacteries. His son stood up to kiss one of the scrolls as he looked on proudly. The scrolls were returned to the Ark, where one of the assistants closed the little doors and drew shut the curtain embroidered with sacred inscriptions. All was peace and comfort—but Herman knew there was no such peace, and that people were threatening them from outside, lurking out there, ready to kill.

He could reconstruct the scene completely in his mind.

The windows of the synagogue flew into pieces. The crystal chandelier swung dangerously above their heads. Panic broke out and the worshippers ran to take refuge around the Ark; then it was silent. Everyone thought the attack was over and began to calm themselves. Herman took his son's hand and went to look for his wife just as someone cried out, pointing toward the broken windows; torch flames were beginning to climb the temple walls. Then everyone scattered out toward the street, where the stormtroopers were waiting for them.

Herman remembered how they had separated him from his wife and son, and he started to cry and beat his breast and strike the bench—because now he also remembered that they had made him dig the ditch to bury those charred bones and that it was there, at that moment, vilified by the Nazis, that he had lost his memory. He felt as lonely as a dog, abandoned in a brutal world where gaining respect no longer mattered. Why didn't they defend themselves? Why did they remain so impassive, without raising a protest?

The memories crowded in on him in a dizzying rush; Herman grew more agitated as the past became clearer. The memory shamed him, because now he felt he was to blame. He reproached himself for submitting so passively to those murderers in grey.

Herman wanted to relive that scene. He wanted to die with them and escape the nightmare he had lived since then. He wanted to return to the year 1941 and the Warsaw ghetto. He wanted another chance.

He was lost in these visions when a noise put him on guard. Someone was moving in the alley behind the synagogue. A light slowly glimmered through the stained glass windows. Out of the depths of the past the whispers became cries and the light multiplied into torch flames coming to burn the temple.

Herman's heart pounded. A cold sweat covered his face, his hands, and his back. The moment for action had arrived.

Once more in his mind the lights of the chandelier went out and his son appeared at his side, pressing against his body, and his wife came running for help, but Herman felt powerless and confused. He knew this was the opportunity he had wished for; it would never come again. He had to meet the challenge or return to his old submission.

The torches were touching the temple walls. Herman began to cry out to his fellow worshippers to stand up and fight, but no one came forward. They were all nailed to their seats, with no spirit to resist. They had surrendered to fatalism.

Suddenly he felt a great rage. He was Herman K.—someone with a name!—and he refused to be intimidated. He had the right to remain a free man, and he wouldn't hand himself over to assassins without a struggle. Seeing his wife and child, he felt he owed them a debt: all at once a great strength surged through him. Through the window he saw the torch's glow and he ran toward it.

He opened the door of the synagogue with a resounding clatter and hurled his gigantic, avenging shadow at the grey phantom waving the torch.

A TRAIN RIDE

Hugo Lindo

Translated by Elizabeth Gamble Miller

As Leonardo Villena strolled along the station platform toward the second-class cars, he inhaled the air with extraordinary gusto. There was always that special aroma of vapors that smelled of a trip. A small briefcase in his left hand was his only baggage. With his right hand he dug into the pocket of his jacket, and, reassured that his ticket was in place, he boarded the train.

The seats in the second-class car were hard, but that didn't seem to matter. He chose one next to a window and sought to entertain himself by looking out. At the moment there wasn't much scenery, unless that's what you would call the yellowed railroad ties piled high like a wall on either side of the tracks. The landscape would later change into meadows and woods, fields of sugar and corn, and little lakes dotted with coveys of wild ducks.

A heavy-set, bald-headed man took the seat beside him and made it immediately clear that he wanted to talk:

"Is your destination La Alianza?"

"No."

"San Esteban?"

"I'm really not going anywhere in particular."

The man was disconcerted, but only for a moment, and then he charged in again:

"Well, I am. I'm going to La Alianza. I've got a whole day of joggling up and down on this foul train. That's where my in-laws are waiting; they're taking care of my little boy while my wife is gone. She's in Miami picking up a few things (lowering his voice to a confidential tone)—contraband, you know."

Leonardo nodded his assent courteously and then directed his attention to lighting a cigarette and taking a deep, long draw.

"They notified me that he got sick, from one day to the next. He's seriously ill, and I have to go to him. I'm really worried, rather upset, you know. I wish the train was almost there."

Leonardo smiled to himself. Everything about the other passenger seemed to be a contradiction: he discussed his anguish with complete composure. He spoke very slowly while explaining his hurry. The man had piqued his interest. For his part he wouldn't try to be aloof or unsociable or to avoid the contact being offered. On the contrary, it was necessary for him to act naturally and even sympathetically. The fact was, he had started the day with a certain pensive disposition, and it was difficult to become engaged in dialogue. He would have to put forth a conscious effort to break down his own noncommunicative shell.

"You say you're not going anywhere in particular. I don't understand."

"I'm just taking a ride. I'll travel until about noon, get off wherever I am and take the next train going west."

"Oh, now I see!"

The car had been filling up with passengers, who were putting their suitcases up, or down in between the seats, or in the passageway, pushing and cursing under their breaths. An atmosphere of ill humor seemed to permeate the air. However, the bad humor around them didn't affect Leonardo Villena or his companion, for they were apparently in another world.

The train whistled, announcing its departure. The men heard the initial asthmatic chugs of the locomotive; that special odor of trains became stronger. They felt the first jerks, heard the squealing of the wheels, and the piles of railroad ties began to move backward, slowly.

"Do you travel like this very often, for pleasure?"

"Not frequently, but when I can. I like trains. Or I should say, I love trains."

"I don't. They bore me; they wear me out. But in a case like this. Just imagine. The poor child, seriously ill and without his mother or his father, depending on his aunts, and what can they do?"

"How old is the boy?" Leonardo asked, in an effort to appear interested.

"Three years old, and an only child. He looks like his mother."

"So much the better!"

The man caught the joke right away and smiled:

"Absolutely! Much better!"

Leonardo's career successes were due to his innate understanding of psychology. He had studied an average amount since entering the university a few years previously. But he had an unusual gift for sizing up people, guessing their intentions, anticipating their actions, and not being caught by surprise. It seemed an appropriate moment to analyze his traveling companion.

As a matter of fact he was rather young. His weight and his baldness contributed to the impression of his being older. This was emphasized by his loose, careless way of dressing. But his small, sharp eyes belied the first impression: there was something about them, a certain innocence, the sign of a rural upbringing; they displayed no tension or malice.

Little by little, the train had picked up speed. The telephone posts sped by and the wires seemed to be suddenly separated and then again united behind the string of cars.

"Don Horacio!"

The greeting was unexpected and enthusiastic. Entering their coach from the second-class car in front of them was a woman. She would have been pretty if it hadn't been for her pronounced nose. Brunette, black eyes, straight hair, a bit fleshy, her appearance was, generally speaking, attractive, although somewhat common. Her only facial feature out of the ordinary was her nose, which made her uglier; however, it also gave her a certain mark of distinction and intelligence.

"Mariita!"

"Where are you bound for?"

Don Horacio—now Leonardo knew his name—repeated the story: the sick child, the absent mother, the aunts, the long, tedious train ride, and above all, the concern for his son. The tremendous worry expressed with a placid face; the uncertain urgency spoken of calmly.

Leonardo Villena again tried to immerse himself in his thoughts, but now the woman had taken the seat directly in front of them and was carrying on a long conversation with Don Horacio. She spoke energetically, affectionately, and with exaggerated gestures. Oh, three-year-olds! So precious! So smart! Something new every minute! So adorable!

Mariita found no lack of expressions of affection for children. One might conclude that she belonged to a society for the protection of children. Villena was engaged in his own thoughts when, without warning, the woman threw a direct question at him:

"And you, sir, have you any children?"

"Yes, I have two."

"Oh, how lovely! How old are they? Are they pretty big now?"

"No. The older one is five. The younger is three."

"Little boys?"

"Yes, they are."

Leonardo thought Mariita was too forward, but his rearing obliged him to answer and not ignore her. Yes, his rearing, a vestige of the bourgeois "teachings" that he had been subjected to by his parents and professors and by the general environment. However, there seemed to be something else involved. It was as if that woman held a strange magnetism for him. She spoke, and he was compelled to pay attention. Besides, her words, though simple enough, carried an undercurrent of emotion that could not be ignored.

He was cognizant of the fact that he should not think about his own children. Certainly not with any emotion. The thought of his boys would of necessity be an inhibiting factor and could jeopardize his mission. No sentimentality, no familial sentimentalism. Nevertheless, it seemed that between them, Mariita and Don Horacio were determined to ruin his plans. He couldn't refrain from thinking of his children. When he had left, they were in bed and he had planted a kiss on each forehead. Fortunately, they were healthy. Because when Leonardito, the older one, caught the measles and was completely covered with bumps, his temperature had risen devilishly high. He had been so worried! Every few minutes he would call the doctor, who could do nothing but prescribe aspirin to lower the fever. Don Horacio, the poor devil, must be feeling the same disquietude, only with his temperament, or perhaps it was just a façade, his anxiety didn't show. But what the devil did he care about Don Horacio and Mariita and the children?

The train made its customary noises as it approached the station:

it blew, whistled, screeched, rumbled, and finally pulled to a stop in front of the station shed at Las Palmas, a shed blackened by trains like all the others in the country, identical to the others in the Americas and even in the world.

One advantage, he said to himself: this interruption will cut off that woman's chitchat and put an end to this man's meddling. He noted his watch. It wasn't time to get off yet. The next station would be the one. But, because of the circumstances, perhaps it would be preferable.

He didn't reveal his intentions, but as he was moving toward the step in order to get off the train, the heavy-set man spied him and called out in a rather demanding voice that attracted everyone's attention:

"Mister! Mister! You're forgetting your valise!"

He thought quickly. If he ran, they would surely go through his briefcase and consequently his mission would fail. If on the other hand he stayed, there would still be time to think up something that would work.

"No, Don Horacio, I'm not leaving. I was just going to get a breath of fresh air."

It was difficult for him to hide his rage and frustration. Why had his seatmates turned out to be precisely these people with their inopportune interference that seemed destined to upset his plans? Like the best actor, he adopted the disguise of being pleasant and relaxed while he cursed his bad luck. He again took his seat and thanked the man for his trouble over the little baggage that he had.

So it was that the train renewed its journey with its tedious, isochronal rhythm, that the woman in a like manner resumed her chatter about children, their charms, their illnesses, the unsettling moments that await their elders, and he was forced to pay even closer attention because of the necessity for dissimulation.

And it was through the small door this attention had opened that the woman's words gradually crept in. With their intense power of suggestion, their incomparable emotional force and subjugating pathos, in spite of the simplicity and domesticity of the thoughts being expressed, her words convinced him: "Hypnotism or something of that order," thought Leonardo Villena for a moment. Just for a moment, because that thought couldn't occupy the same space being reclaimed by his home. The warm images emerged from behind that prominent nose through the strange voice of Mariita and those steady, unavoidable, demanding eyes that shone like precious stones. "Absurd," he thought instantly. And then again he saw Leonardito burning up with fever, his little head wet with perspiration lying on the pillow and moving about restlessly, just the way this fat man's son must be doing now in La Alianza—the son of his gentle traveling companion.

"Traveling companion"—something clicked in his memory as the phrase crossed his mind. Possible; he was not sure. He did begin to consider that at least for the moment his mission was inopportune. Rather than the government, its victims would be the anonymous train passengers. Perhaps even more than them, the injury would be to that unknown child, his traveling companion's son—the boy who might be Leonardito's traveling companion at some future date.

Exerting his willpower, he shook his head and succeeded in uttering one word, "foolishness," but the word was swallowed up in a great black tunnel mysteriously taking shape as he saw before him Mariita's eyes and, deep within, like a drop of gleaming water, the flash of innocence.

He could not complete his mission.

Old houses with crumbling walls moved slowly across the train window. Cows were mooing. Wire fences etched stripes into the landscape. And then came the school yard with its children, lots of children, noisy children whose cries penetrated the railroad car. The train stopped moving and Leonardo found it the opportune moment to escape that diabolical pair. He grabbed his briefcase, muttering to himself the word "traitor," and made his way off the train.

PENELOPE ON HER SILVER WEDDING ANNIVERSARY

Rima Vallbona

Translated by Barbara Paschke

To the woman who has
dissociated herself from
the society of Pharisees

Preparations for the party have created an atmosphere of anxiety among the inhabitants of the house. And it's not even an upper-class snob who's coming! At best, something will happen that will make history in this sleepy town. As for myself, I feel uneasy as the hours of the day vainly move around to accommodate themselves to my normal working rhythms, but it's impossible. Habitual routine has been abandoned, known limits have been broken, everything is rolling toward something unexpected, and... damn, what will it be? Will something really happen?

A party's just a party, old man, relax, don't let your nerves tense up like violin strings quivering through all the recesses of your carcass at the slightest sound of the dishes being carefully washed by Jacinta, the old maid.

"I, who held her in my arms when she was still a little bit of nothing, look at her now. I never thought I'd endure so much, so much, throughout my life! I would never have believed it!" continues Jacinta, whispering her litany through the dark spaces between her few spotless teeth, while in the basin, amidst spurts of water, she creates an orchestration of china, crystal, and silver. Moreover, that unbearable odor of garlic and fried food is impregnating the atmosphere; it's already penetrated me to the bone and here I am fatigued with a hell of a case of nausea and I don't know if it's from the food or, well, from what's going to happen today.

Those noises, those culinary odors mixed with the penetrating aromas of jasmine, wildflowers, roses, gardenias, bringing up a knot of nausea in my stomach, creating distances between things that before I always manipulated unreservedly, almost with disdain. It's as if things were becoming more and more sacred and I were desecrating them. Taking the coffee spoon, I had to let it go with a certain superstitious move. Blasted nausea! I felt the cigarette I was going to light come alive in my mouth and I dropped it, lacking the energy to lift it.

Charito and Laura are singing while making the beds; spreading out the clean white sheets, dazzling in the morning light, their young arms draw magic, impossible sails in the air, that raise in me, disconnected here in this armchair, the desire to enter into their intimate circle of laughter and song and soak up all their kisses. "They are your cousins, your little orphan cousins whom you have to love and respect forever. You're evil, Abelardo, what you've done will earn you the pain of hell. You have to confess and never do it again." How smooth and tender their skin was underneath the water in the river. Never again in my life have I had such a full and complete sensation of paradise: the multicolored vegetation falling headlong into the water in a transcendental suicide of branches mottled with parasites, rushes, and vines. And the silence punctured by a thousand noises, bursting in the cry of the cicada or in the ripe mango's splitting as it falls on the ground. And in the murmur of the river, the murmur of blood swollen with healthy new pleasures. "Pain of hell. Mortal sin." It was paradise, Mama, the same paradise that had blossomed magically when I was fourteen. That flavor of damp virgin skin, bearing the same invitation to be bitten as a fresh apple. Their small pubescent bodies rolling, swollen with pleasure in the waves of the river. I closed my eyes and let myself go, let myself go, let myself go. . . . They allowed me to penetrate into the atmosphere that wrapped their young arms and legs around my body like a fleshy net, and there I surrendered to the magic comforts of those long nights spent trying to ease the hard pain between my legs, that pain that made me so ashamed. It was paradise. Hell consisted of nights that hardened my bed, when fearfully I had to bear the swelling of sin. That was hell.

But Mama, the poor thing, she was so good! Never understood nor understands now that everything isn't just games, bicycles, marbles, desks, books, and two times two equals four. For her, the armchair next to the window and the two needles that never tire of knitting, knitting, knitting, always knitting. She's waiting for something. I know she's waiting for something. Each rapid, nervous movement of her needle says that she's waiting for something. But she's been waiting so long! And what has she knit during that long time? She must have a room full of bedspreads, slippers, undershirts, cushions, sweaters, hats, scarves. Where does she put all those things she knits? Today, with the hustle and bustle and preparations for the party—damned party that's put me in such a mood—I think with uneasiness about those weavings of Mama's. How strange! Where does she keep them if I've never seen her use them or give them away? Could there be a secret room in the house? Where? White wool. Always white wool, with no hint of color at all. Ever since I was a child I saw her knitting by the window and humming a melancholy song that had the lilt of a waltz; afterwards, she covered me with kisses that trembled with anguish. "Why do you knit so much, Mama?" She kept on humming, and a tear rolled down her cheek every time I asked her the question. "Where's the white sweater you knit last week?" She rose from the chair in silence and went to see if Jacinta had dinner ready or if she had made the tortillas. I always asked her, but I had never before thought about Mama like today, nor about her strange knitting. Ever since I heard her speak and understood her words, all she said was sin, pain of hell, evil, and afterwards, as if she had never entered into the magic circle of flesh pregnant with pleasure, she pronounced only everyday words: sausage, sauces, tamales, beans, cleanliness, do the wash, water the periwinkles and carnations, knit. "I have to knit. I have to finish these slippers." When she says "I have to," a tombstone settles over her being, burying everything that seemed alive while she was stirring the pot of vegetables or mixing the cornmeal for tamales.

When she hears a love song or a finch warbling, something is immediately stirred up inside her—at least it seems so to me—something that reminds me of the magic circle of my cousins, as if through two doors an unexpected paradise were half opened to her. But then she continues talking about the same things, as if life were nothing but routine and daily chores. Papa impassively accepts her conversation. No, it's not conversation. She throws together words that seem to be conversation, but not conversation. The strange thing is that her every word comes out as if whatever she's naming were held in her mouth.

"Leave her in her own world, Abelardo, she's happy that way, in her simple woman's world. Twenty-five years of marriage and never a complaint or reproach. She's happy knitting. She's happy among the pots and pans in the kitchen, arranging flowers, rearranging the furniture. If our man's world were like a woman's, everything would be a bed of roses. Look, look at the gray hair I have from being bent over my desk."

Mama has no gray hair, but her eyes seem to contain a gravestone that entombs all life inside her. In the morning, when she gets up, her complexion has a strange moistness, as if the night's dew had watered the soft furrows that are now beginning to be outlined around her eyes. Not one gray hair. Her clean, shining, reddish-brown hair gathered into an elegant chignon. When she isn't talking about all that everyday nonsense, she seems like a regal figure out of a painting in a museum. But as she goes about pronouncing daily details ("the soup came out delicious") in the soft singsong of her hometown, her skin turns into a vile, worthless material, I get the urge to gag her and hide her in a corner, the urge to cover my ears so I can continue to see her as regal and beautiful. Why the devil don't you get away from your banana, cabbage, sauces, plants...? Ah, Mama, Mama. How ashamed I feel when my friends come by and you in front of them with your eyes the tomatoes spoiled and the lettuce is tender. They look at me, shrug their shoulders without understanding the simplicity of your world, and keep on talking to me about everything that makes you shrug your shoulders in disdain.

Why the party today? Why? Why does it worry me so? One more party, like all the others. That knot of nausea is now in my throat. Will more knitting fit into Mama's room full of knitting? Does she intend to continue there by the window, white wool, white wool, white wool? Nights at the opera at the National Theater, entranced by the brilliance of the chandeliers. Dancing until your shoes wear out and taking along another pair to finish off the night.... When did she say that? No, she never said that. I dreamed it in one of those children's dreams which are so easily confused with reality. "And my dance program always made the others jealous. Everyone wanted to dance with me." A vague sensation of having heard it from her lips. Perhaps it wasn't she. Someone, any one of those vain old women who come to visit her and talk like real chatterboxes. White wool, the kitchen—nausea, nausea—it's her world, small, ridiculously unimportant, from which she never steps out. Poor little thing. Like grandma and like all women, with no wings to fly toward the infinite horizon, with no dreams to conquer.... Bah! Idiocy. It's absurd, including that room with the knitting. This fragile little woman who has the consistency of a shadow for all the emptiness she has inside. How crazy can I get!

Charito's skin is warm and vibrant against my thighs, but it slips away from me like a live fish... it's so tender pressed tightly against me, palpitating ardently, endlessly, and protecting her beautiful perverted virginity! The pain of hell, evil, the only different things she ever said, because she couldn't understand what happens with Charito when her skin brushes against mine and we meld ourselves infinitely. Mama knows nothing about this. Has she felt it even once with Papa... with anyone? Impossible; she's different, as if she lived for nothing but white wool and the kitchen. Strange. When the history teacher talked about the Tinoco dictatorship, the orgies and madness, she, Mama, was there in my imagination, lively and smiling, hair beautifully curled, with a gleaming, ample décolletage, "and Pelico Tinoco wanted to seduce me, as well, but I..." It's absurd! She isn't that old and besides she's my mother, which is only to say...

Time for the party. The guests are coming in, and little by little the posturing, the lying, and the gossip are solidifying in the open spaces between bodies. Laughter, words, embraces, and kisses have lost their essence and their reality. For a while I'm weighed down—nausea, more nausea—with the fear that Mama's mouth will start to fill up with banana, sauces, stew, tamales. She's so beautiful, all dressed in black, which makes the red in her hair stand out. Regal as ever. But just don't let her speak, just let her keep going without touching on mundane reality.

What? What are they saying? That she's going to make a public announcement? Everyone's looking at her. Papa is aghast. This is a nightmare. She has never spoken like this, in public. Among all these flesh-eating vulture-people, how did it occur to her to be so ridiculous? My God, Mama! Why did you have a drink if you can't hold your liquor, did the alcohol make you giddy? Come with me. No, I want to say something important to all my friends. Leave me alone, Abelardo, and tell your father that I haven't had even a sip. Mama, my dear, for the love of God, keep quiet.

She stood up on a stool and majestically and with authority made everyone be still. She had the most marvelous regal gestures. If only she could have stayed that way forever and never spoken....

My dear friends, you who have accompanied us through these twenty-five years of marriage, today I want to be sincere with all of you for the first time. How could I celebrate our twenty-five years of marriage, our silver anniversary, today without sharing with all of you *my* happiness? (Did she say *my* happiness that way, emphasizing the "my"? And Papa's? She's drunk. She's not used to champagne, which goes right to your head.)

Do you know what these twenty-five years of my life have been like, living with an egotistical, cruel, foolish, and lascivious man? (Crazy, she's crazy, drunk, the champagne, the things she's saying!) Do you know the nights of insomnia and the days of backbreaking work I have spent by his side? (A dream, a nightmare. She isn't really saying this, she doesn't know and never did know how to express anything. She's drunk. Get her out of here.) No, I'm not going to tell you about each and every tear I shed during those twenty-five years. What are you all whispering about down there? I'm only going to tell you why I'm happy and content today. Why am I celebrating these twenty-five years? My son, Abelardo, is now grown and no longer needs me. And neither does my husband. What I'm celebrating today is my freedom. Have you ever seen a prisoner after he's completed his sentence and regained his freedom? That prisoner is me. (I can't stand any more, the house is falling down on top of me.) Today I want to announce that I'm declaring myself free from the yoke of matrimony, free to spend my time however I please. I'm going to treat myself to traveling all over the world. No more of those little vacations to Playa del Coco or Puerto Limon or Puntarenas, where he took me after taking his mistresses to Acapulco, Capri, and Biarritz. (Crazy, crazy, crazy...!) The best part of today is to be able to break forever the silence of twenty-five years in which I was becoming a breeding ground for worms. Let's drink, my friends, to the freedom that today is my happiness and my husband's as well.... (Papa, poor Papa, what shame!) Because isn't it true, dear, that it's a relief that I've said it and you didn't have to? That way, I'm the scandalous one and you can stay the same as always, virtuous before the world. Like always. Let's toast contentedly, without rancor or hatred, content like the good friends we've always been.

The sensation of being in an unreal atmosphere which had pursued me since morning gathered such force that I thought I was a victim of the many martinis I had drunk. Once again I had the strange impression that there were sacred distances between myself and other things; those material things that previously palpitated as soon as I saw them now disappeared from view, resisted touch, slipped away, disappeared in a horrible nightmare.

Mama was on the stool and went on talking. It was then I realized that her beautiful black dress had a very provocative neckline. Her neck—I'd never thought about it before—is firm and fresh like Charito's and still exciting.... No! What am I thinking, she's my mother! She's laughing and laughing lustfully with that attractive gray-haired man; they're burying their looks in each other, all those things I can't even imagine the two of them are saying. The martinis.... I'm drunk. She, Papa, twenty-five years, the anniversary, that man: Dr. Garcés, yes, it's Dr. Garcés, the one who took care of her during her long illness. He saved her life... now he's saving her from... pain of hell... evil, she's evil like all women... they're talking with their eyes... and Papa? It's all the martinis' fault, I don't even know who I am.

She can't—mustn't—break the monotonous rhythm of sauce, tamales, yucca... pain of hell... she must keep knitting next to the window. I'll buy her all the white wool necessary to completely close up that sinful neckline and so she won't have time to look that way at Dr. Garcés. She was born for knitting.

I still have a little bit of life left to enjoy; the rest of my life is for me alone. Why not now while there's still time? The time of slavery is now past. (Pain of hell. It's evil. She's looking at Dr. Garcés like Charito looks at me when our flesh is saturated with each other. She, too, my mother, clean, pure, tireless knitter of useless things. Hell is this torture today, not the river, not the arms of Charito and Laura... I thought that...)

Everything became still more unreal when she began bringing out all the articles of clothing that she had knit, white wool, white, white wool, and distributing them among all the guests. Then the unexpected happened: everyone got carried away in their intoxication and began putting on their knitted clothing until they all were crazily costumed in wool, white, white wool. They grew in the midst of so much wool, and under the shining lights, everyone collapsed in a white mass of multiple arms and legs that trembled in a crazy din of freedom and lust.

AN ANTISTORY

Alvaro Menéndez Franco

Translated by Leland H. Chambers

Saturday. In Panama the days of the week each have their personality. But... why begin my story this way? I could begin with another plot. Let's see: The beaches of the Pacific Ocean are grazing against the shores of the city. In Las Bóvedas a hundred or so well-dressed children are skating. Their faces are bright red from the effort. There are also other children, prematurely old, who go around with their bare feet on the ground: filthy, hair wild and abundant; bodies covered with sores; flaccid and anemic. Their faces are emaciated and their eyes show the granitic anguish of not having what others do. The certainty of growing up to be a newsboy on the streets, and nothing more. The painful reality of rising with the sun and, stiff with cold, shouting at the top of their lungs to offer their newsy merchandise. Okay... but why not begin my story in another way? I'm absolutely convinced that a lot of people will accuse me of being a demagogue. After all, "Here in Panama there has been so much lying that when someone wants to tell the truth no one believes it." There are many motives for writing. For that very reason, to imitate is absurd. I could write about the Panamanian rural folk. People worn away by parasitic disease, endemic goiter, and pernicious anemia. They live badly and die badly. Sometimes you're not sure whether the order of things is the same for them as it is for us. Perhaps, for them, dying is living, because they are freed from misery, from their truncated, dark existence. Frankly, I believe that the peasant plays out his life with a machete in his hand because he knows his life's worth nothing. All you have to do is make a list: a sun that dehydrates, a scorched land without nutrients, earth from which you stubbornly and suicidally pull something; politicians who sell you a couple of candles and a cemetery plot and then buy your vote. All right then, but why are you going on to some other page without reading my story? I'm convinced you're just like all the others who don't believe in misery because you've never known it yourself. I'm sure you believe in God without knowing him. So what are you talking about? Faith? Nonetheless, the peasant believes in his machete more than faith, although during Holy Week he goes to the villages to kiss the saints' feet, the paint faded and flaked off from the passing of time. But what are you doing interfering with my story? You shouldn't interfere. I'm writing this story without anyone's help. If you argue with me you're helping me to write it. You ought to just stick to reading it. That's all. Your conclusions? They don't interest me. Although of course it seems to me that one writes for others, not for one's self, egoistically. That doesn't mean you have the right to argue with me and tell me your ideas. You're probably just one of those café geniuses who spend the whole day talking about Raimundo and all the rest of the world. You say *you* are a peasant? Please, don't make me laugh....

You were born in Antón? Are you the kind of person who thinks being born in the interior is all it takes to consider yourself a peasant? You're sadly mistaken. Now I ask you please to let me write my story. If you don't like it, go somewhere else. You can find your girlfriend and go to a movie. Or maybe you can go to the beach and take a swim. Anyway, I'm determined to write my story, and nothing and no one is going to stop me. I've already begun it twice. Don't you think I have a right to think this idea through carefully? It isn't possible to write foolishness. I hope you're thinking of going. Good.

A lot of people are just like this guy: they start to read something and never finish it. They go off to watch a ball game, spend hours beneath the dog-day sun, shouting until they're hoarse, and afterward they leave, discussing every little detail of the game. Meanwhile, set them to reading a book and they don't even read the title!

Saturday. Days in Panama... (better make that everywhere). Where's the eraser? Better to cross out and write above. Of course, every day has its peculiarities. For example, on Tuesdays a lot of people go in search of a woman to read the cards for them. If it's Sunday, you have to go to the race track, and it doesn't matter that the kids will go hungry tomorrow. On Saturdays the Avenida Central fills with waves of humanity. Everyone looking for a lottery ticket! There's no lack of U.S. sailors, euphoric, shouting, going from bar to bar, cabaret to cabaret. I remember very well when there were still cars in the city. They used to rent them and would go up and down all the streets shouting, happy to find themselves in a country where "everything"—apparently—"is so green." Happy slot machines, movie theaters, whorehouses. Cantinas, cantinas, cantinas. Women and taxis. "Green Panama."

What *we* know about, what we're familiar with, is it green? I'll lay odds, two to one, that no one can demonstrate that the Chorillo districts are green, or that the yards in the Barrio del Marañón are green. The only green thing in Panama is the disgrace stuffed into the pockets of certain members of the ruling class. Gangsters of the vote, of surrender. You have to go into the interior of the country to see whether peasants without land see life with the color of hope. On the contrary: they see it black. They leave their blood on the floors of the black cantinas after having fought with their black-handled machetes, after black visions of fear and rage have passed before their eyes. But that's the way it is. I'm writing a story, and I would like it to be very beautiful for whoever reads it. But writing is no easy thing. Sometimes you feel like putting away your pencil and deceiving yourself by saying you'll go on writing later. I've done that with lots of stories. They're all half finished. I don't know. Maybe I'm being disloyal to my readers, because I don't write for myself, but for them. I've begun this story three times. The truth is, in this atmosphere, nothing stimulates you. I go out. I walk along Tres de Noviembre street. It's nighttime. In a vestibule beneath a town house, a group of men are buying some fried food. A rather elderly woman waits on them. I turn the corner. Now I'm going along the

Avenida Central. Saturday: I see faces and more faces. Now I find myself on Santa Ana. I haven't an inkling of an inspiration. It's difficult to write a story. Let's see, I could write about a prostitute. But a lot of writers have written about that. "Rodríguez" is a story with that theme. Fito Aguilera wrote it. I'd like to write a story on the order of Changmarín's "Six Mothers." It's a great story. I also like Ramón H. Jurado's "Stone." Right now I don't know what to write. I get up. Better have a drink. Maybe a spark will come along to start something going. Sitting in the Cosmopolitan Bar. A drink. Another, and still another. I've lost count. My eyelids feel heavy. A terrible thirst.

Ah, but what do I see? It's the idiot I was arguing with. "Come on over." The man draws closer without speaking. He doesn't seem to recognize me.

"How's it going, how are you? Did you like the game?"

"What game?"

"The ball game, man. Don't you remember we were having an argument this morning? I was writing a story and you wouldn't leave me alone. . . ."

The man looks surprised. His eyes betray confusion, and there's a slight, nervous trembling at the corners of his mouth.

"Excuse me, but I don't know you. . . . What is your name?"

"My name's fam... fam... Ha ha ha! Those are the words to a *guaracha*. Did you know that in these cantinas you don't hear *guarachas* anymore?

The man looks at me, even more put off. I can see him trying to coordinate his thoughts. He has a common-looking face, very simple. It would be interesting to write about this simple type. The truth is that not many people write about the people they call "ordinary," the man in the street. I can invite him to have a drink. Then I'll get him into a conversation to see what he says. It's a good topic to write about. You can't always be inventive.

"Sit down, my friend. Something to drink?"

"No thanks. I have to go."

He turns away from me.

There goes my story, walking out of the cantina.

HIGH NOON IN APRIL

Julio Escoto

Translated by Alberto Huerta

Day broke. General Fernández sprang like a tiger from his canvas cot, and the coarse maguey blanket, saturated with sweat from the feverish night, slid to the dirt floor. He got up and immediately sensed the pain over his jawbone, cutting into his wisdom tooth sharply like glass. He moved his hand to his face, but instinct stopped it in the air and he lowered it consciously to his side to see if he still had the pistol with which he had slept through a night of silent lament, guarded by the anxious eyes of his followers, who were gathered beyond sleep and the suspicion of death. Inside the tent, the oozing of bodily smells mixed with the copious aroma of mint ointment floated through the air, and a yellowish mist of dust shone through the silent walls held behind the last wink of the sun. General Fernández staggered lightly in his riding boots, balancing himself with difficulty between the vapors of suffocation and the first sudden blasts of an early watch loaded with heat and thirst.

"Damn it," he said, thinking about the comet while he walked to the entrance, "they forgot reveille, the sons of bitches."

He slapped open the mosquito net and lifted the dust flap of the tent. A flood of light that reeked of salt invaded the small chamber, scattering its rays over the empty ammunition boxes, the washbasin covered with the remains of dead mosquitoes, the field maps rolled in tin cylinders, and the saddle with silver rivets and stirrups of hard *guayaco* wood attached to a halter. A locust jumped three times and fluttered fleetingly across his face. The general spat on the rough, wrinkled bed sheet stained with the same volcanic silica that poured out of the stitching of his boots.

The first thing he saw in the distance, through the waxy glare of April that laid waste to the plum trees and deadened the activity of the beehives, was the reddish iron slag of his three field cannons. Their bases were raised toward the mountain range, while their muzzles pointed toward the tent where he had just been ruminating about the penance of a wisdom tooth wrapped with chewing tobacco and lime paste. When he had focused his sight, blurred by the hellish haze of heat that covered the plain, he realized that what he had never thought would happen to him in the wildest imaginings of his worst nightmares had happened. He was alone. They had left him all alone on the dawn of his day of victory, the eve of the last battle, up against the wall of his own misfortunes and under the faded regalia of the illusions of power that had no name. Damn, he cursed, scaring the iguanas that crawled under his cot. He took out a guard rifle, which his big hands swung in the air as if it were an accordion. Such an inconsiderate act wasn't done to the president of the Republic. He fired three rounds into the thin pine partition. Pigs, he stammered, his throat tightening with sulfurous indignation.

Upon hearing the gunshots, his followers came quickly, still enveloped by the rose-hued dawn. Holding up their trousers, adjusting their suspenders, and wearing their tight goatskin leggings, they moved through a dense cloud of clinging dust that patted their shoulders, whitened their moustaches, and made them sneeze. Commander, they said, Sir, what's the matter, all you need to do is give us the order. But the general eyed them from a distance through many layers of mistrust. Jackasses. They weren't aware of the mass desertion. If they would only look at their ranks, which had been husked like corn, and in which they had put hope during their sleep. Soldiers of the fatherland, he lamented, a light moving enemy for soldiers made of lead. Never, no more votive candles to the Virgin. What had happened was that they had become careless. While the nest egg was being robbed, the birdfaces had been asleep and we were left without soldiers or militia, the gunners daydreaming, the lookouts caught napping. Indolent, that's what they were. Don't think about it, Sir. Right now they would reorganize the army. They would go out and capture volunteers, recruit peasants. They would go out to convince the deserters to return.

"What's the problem, *compadre?*"[1] Colonel Sanabria entered, his spurs clanging as he fastened the swagger stick to his belt. General Fernández turned to look at him. In the cordial distance between the two men there was an electric charge of energy that sparked the poles of suspicion. And even if they had established the familial ties that come from ritual ceremonies, and even if in previous campaigns against the guerillas they had shared the same trenches, the same women, the same riches of the State, their two ambitions didn't fit into the same room. Both had the same virtue of disturbing each other's sleep and flooding each other's defenses by feigning friendly traps, effective blunders, and diplomatic rivalries. The warm splendor of an assassin's love always glittered in their official embraces, a love they knew how to manipulate and enjoy, and with which both were naturally gifted.

When the general saw the colonel, he felt the sharp pain in his tooth. He turned his back, even though he sensed the chilling stare of the colonel, who had the body of a huge bull and was crisscrossed with the scars of three bayonet wounds he had received in the mountains of Acajutla. The general quickly opened his tobacco case and extracted two fingers' worth of the weed, which he mixed with a pinch of lime and placed in the cavity of his mouth. He gently tightened his jaw without hinting at any pain, especially in the presence of his *compadre*. He slowly began to feel the moisture of the paste and the doughy taste of the tobacco juice that bathed the gum. Its placid warmth made him secrete a spontaneous bubble of spittle; he rinsed his mouth with it and then spat it out.

Colonel Sanabria was examining the bullet holes that had punctured the floral designs of the pinewood partition when General Fernández cursed:

"Cowards," he said with clenched teeth, his eyes burning with a hatred that made them look like two diamond cuff links, "the same as when we fought in the gorge at Zelaya. Everyone fled because they were afraid of the enemy."

"We've gone through some bad times together," Sanabria added, without trying to balance the weight of the double meaning, "but we survived. That time we also won. So don't be discouraged, my *compadre* president." He patted his shoulder. "Right now I'll get them back for you—that is, if you give me a little time and permission to execute a few as an example, just like the last time."

General Fernández, reflecting, responded with only a grunt. Last time it had been by ministerial decree and by his own hand. Was Sanabria now trying to score a few points with public opinion? If he gave in, it would look as if Sanabria had been the one to carry out the order correctly, following official regulations. And after all, what mattered most in the eyes of the lawyers in Congress was that regulations were followed. If he disapproved, the guerrillas could come and find them without arms, without men, and without power. The colonel seemed to read in the air the unfolding of these secret thoughts.

"*Compadre,*" Sanabria explained gently, with the conviction that he had all the cards in his hand, "we believe what we want to believe, but realities impose themselves."

"Your stupid talk of history again," interrupted the general. His declaration jarred the wad of tobacco from its place. He arched his tongue toward the back of his mouth and replaced the wad. "It's not time to recall the Greeks again." He chewed lightly. "Go on," he ordered, "I'll give you three hours to put the reins of another army into my hands."

Colonel Sanabria clicked his heels so noisily that he shook the caked dust covering the shine on his spurs. He went out, touching his pistol with his fingertips and glancing quickly to each side of the tent. Outside he gulped down a salty blow of the sun.

"And turn the cannons around, *compadre,*" he heard the general yell at him. The colonel smiled with perverse delight. "Fucked," he thought, wryly, "those unfortunate deserters."

Exhausted, General Fernández dropped on the old cot he had inherited from the last intervention of the Marines. Was it the heat coming in or the fever rising again? He unbuttoned his shirt and opened his uniform. A blast of hot air smelling of tobacco made the hairs on his chest dance, but he turned his face with repugnance from his own breath. "The man who chews tobacco isn't far from eating shit," he mused. Nobody smoked or drank in his presence. A theosophist couldn't permit such bodily pleasures, which rotted the mind. His government had striven for the conciliation of the spirit and the flesh, but only when it involved the reform of Indian customs, instruction in the gifts of obedience, and the acceptance of peace. He thought, if it weren't for the guerrillas, who had resisted his offer of civilization with four years of attacks and bombings, what a sea of tranquility he would have. In his sixteen years of command, they were the most dangerous of all who had dared to raise a fist, to defy his reasons of state with liberal talk of free elections and human rights. Did they know that they were human beings?

He got up and with two sudden pulls opened the straps of his boots. He then went to a corner of the tent and began to rummage through bundles of documents, notebooks with paper seals, facsimiles of decrees, and copies of treaties in leather pouches and cotton covers. He set apart the little mahogany box, with its decorations and engraved designs of doves in flight, and found the demitasse cups. He took the album and blew away the film of dust that was beginning to cover it and form a crusted layer of volcanic earth. These were his love poems, secret voices written only for the music of two: the chosen and himself. As he tenderly caressed the manifestation of that hidden vocation, his heart and his wisdom tooth felt pain at the same time. He took the porcelain demitasse cups and poured into them the multicolored water from an opaque jug. He tripped over the ammunition boxes while emptying the water from one cup into another, desperately trying to inhale the oxygen that broke open from the rose-colored and violet bubbles.

It was true. He calmed down and reflected that there had been bad times but also good ones. He didn't feel much self-pity about the two attempts on his life, even though he did harbor an all but extinguished anger, a minuscule ember of passion, because they had placed the poison in his toast glass at the banquet. It was an error in basic diplomatic courtesy not to let him finish his dinner of splendid partridges and steaming tamales. The other attempt wasn't worth the scar of memory: the stick of dynamite disguised as a candle on his birthday cake was an unfortunate act of the crudest imagination. If the chorus had delayed one more second and if he hadn't put out the candles with such a strong puff, he would have been blown to smithereens, his atoms mixing with the sweet frosting of the cake and the cream of the rice pudding. That attempt was offensive to his dignity, and he preferred to forget it. The disorderly flight of the insurgents after their foiled coup had been such that it was necessary to classify them as "tourists abroad" in order to quiet speculations from the foreign press—a press whose propensity was always to see in his every act the odious mania of a dictator.

What did they know about his duty to civilize? Only his *compadre* could understand the magnitude of the mission on which they had embarked. And that was in spite of his *compadre's* ridiculous passion for Greek history, which made him show off his pedantry by citing famous dates or by assuming the gestures and postures of a tropical tragedian. "Beware the Ides of March," he had said—the clown didn't realize that it was from a Roman ballad. But even if it had been a fluke, Sanabria's premonitions paid off. After the uprising of San Miguel, he had advised the general, "We must negotiate."

"Negotiate! You must be crazy. Negotiate with the insurgents! Whose side are you on?" he had said, accusingly.

"We must negotiate," he repeated. "There are too many of them—there are thousands, *compadre*." The general was on the verge of having him arrested and buried in the dark dungeons of the central fortress when Sanabria added discreetly, "We have time, *compadre*, we have time to dispatch the army and position our cannons on top of the lookouts and make them into potato salad, reduce them to puree." He rubbed his hands with malicious delight.

And during the seven days that Sanabria led the bombardment of the city, he punctually sent the general a rose for every hanged rebel along with little messages proclaiming the brotherly faith with which he was defending the Constitution. When Fernández received him in the Cathedral Square for the victory parade, he teased him: "*Compadre*, you are an animal. You have blotted an entire city from the map for me, exterminator."

"I am the instrument of God," Sanabria had answered, chewing his words behind the dried wrinkles of military exhaustion. "I am your right hand, *compadre*." The two embraced and wept before the compassionate gaze of the Bishop and the many bouquets of roses that flooded the altar.

General Fernández heard footsteps outside his tent, the movements of recruits, the neighing of horses, and the unloading of gear. He anticipated, "They are returning. One by one, they are returning."

After the uprising of San Miguel, however, he had had to pay up. Congress asked him for permission to award Colonel Sanabria the highest medal of the National Condor, exempting him, of course, from the clause stipulating death in combat. The cowed lawyers shook with emotion from the boldness of their initiative and from the joy of his presence—a presence that enveloped them in an atmosphere charged with intense animal charisma. That was the first time he had considered the truth of that recurrent dream: to give his *compadre* the Cross of Cedar, but to give it postmortem. Now he had to deal with these sycophantic skinheads who proposed to shoot higher than his modest ambitions.

"Tradition, my dear colleagues, tradition," he began. Like sponges the lawyers soaked up the colored plumage of his most polished egalitarian manners. "Tradition imposes its own sacred organizational goal; the entire hierarchy will be in the hands of the citizen with the highest decoration." The full Congress yielded, apprehensive of his hidden message. Both men received their respective decorations at the awards ceremony. "I defended you with a sword and you pay me back with a stick," Colonel Sanabria complained, as the Cross of Cedar was pinned to his uniform. "*Compadre*, the best gift I can give you is the realization that you still have some ambition left," he answered in a whisper, while smiling for the photographers.

"Excuse me, Sir, permission to pass," said the aide-de-camp from the edge of the hazy sun which stretched beyond the mosquito net. "Volunteers are arriving, Sir," explained the soldier as he snapped to attention, without looking directly at him sitting on the cot. "Sir, they are enlisting with much enthusiasm." General Fernández made a slight gesture of approval and fanned the air toward the entrance. The soldier marched out, holding in his breath.

But during the last several years, the rancorous soup that inflamed their friendship had begun to cool. They were getting old and their mutual apprehension was softening. The private parties where women were auctioned on the sofas of diplomatic drawing rooms became more and more frequent. They were substituting sex for the drive for power. They were getting old, and he suspected that what Sanabria longed for from the Greeks was the taste of wine more than the entanglements of philosophy. The colonel traveled a lot and always returned with strange ideas, improbable inventions, fantasies of other worlds that couldn't possibly exist in the way he said they did. "If what you tell me about the world is true, it's becoming liberal," he once said to him. "I'll bet you it is, *compadre*," Sanabria replied. Years ago it wouldn't have occurred to him to believe what he saw.

The last thing Colonel Sanabria had dropped into Fernández's little sack of suspicion had occurred during the uprising of the sharecroppers. Rumors had begun to spread around the province of Morazán that the agitators were mobilizing their forces and brainwashing the populace into nonconformity. "Take care of the problem," the general had tersely ordered the provincial commanders, but the itch continued to spread like wildfire, corroding and destroying everything, undermining the foundation of the government he had laboriously built. Large numbers of the secret police were confused by the many rumors and the possibility of further outbreaks, which went beyond the limits of their fears. The mayors came and the governors returned; every morning posters appeared. The women refused to make love to the soldiers in the barracks so that they wouldn't be caught off guard. Orders were given and then contradicted. Ominous black vultures flew over Morazán.

By the end of the week, Colonel Sanabria had returned in haste from abroad and rushed to the president's office immediately upon landing. General Fernández was standing in front of the picture window, watching the sun set over the voluminous gardenias and bananas in flower and contemplating in the distance the walls of a city without a sea. December strung beads of frozen water, and the cavernous mouth of the sleeping volcano exhaled a cold north wind that rattled the windows. The general sensed an air of circumspection in the room.

"What do the foreign newspapers have to say?" he asked, without turning around.

"Bad. Everything is bad," answered the colonel, observing the hunched back, the slumped shoulders, and the ring of fat around the president's waist that looked as if he were embracing a rattlesnake or were a circus woman or an automobile tire. "They call it the barefoot rebellion," he continued, "and they say that your government's time is almost up."

"You mean our government," the general corrected, as he turned to face him. The brilliance of the setting sun reflected in the windows formed a huge light, a monstrous aura of consummate will, and for the first time Colonel Sanabria felt the distance that comes from making fatal decisions. A man more powerful than himself spoke, a man called to meet at will all the faces of death, a man whose cruelty was unfathomable.

"The rebellion is really about ideas, *compadre*," explained the Colonel, "not about men. The rebels are a product of the times, of the changes that come about. If we are to survive, we have to adapt ourselves and conquer by changing, win by transforming."

"Just ideas, eh, *compadre?*" responded the general, sarcasm dripping from his lower lip. "And the newspapers call it the barefoot rebellion. Great!" He pouted with renewed determination. Never had Colonel Sanabria seen him surrounded by such a phosphorescent halo of tranquility and anger. He thought that this man was destiny itself.

There was a long, drawn-out silence in which the president scribbled something with the big round pen on his desk. He neither breathed nor raised his eyes nor felt the passage of time.

"We are going to vaccinate the barefoot against the rebellion," he said at last, calling his secretary and handing him the scribbled note for a telegram. "Go in peace, *compadre*. We are going to have a peaceful Christmas," he added, as he dismissed him.

"What are you going to do, *compadre?*" he dared to ask, his hand on the doorknob. He wasn't afraid for himself. He was afraid because the general's heart was flooded with hate that was drowning him. The silence bounced crazily between the four walls and shattered into fragments of darkness.

"The people love me," murmured the general to himself as he faced the picture window again. "The barefoot love me because I have given them everything," he repeated in a convinced monologue. "The educated and the cultured are the ones who are against me, those who have already gotten ahead, those who read and learn to repeat liberal slogans. The people, indeed, love me."

Colonel Sanabria went out into the darkness, hat in hand. Outside, the secretary, his eyes wild, was waiting for him. He took the paper that was trembling in his hands. "Execute everyone wearing shoes," he read. The general's black scribbling emerged like the imprint of a hairy spider.

"It was true. That's how everything had happened," reflected the general as he arose from his cot. But the sharp jab in his tooth forced him to sit down. He was dizzy with pain. With his eyes half closed he prepared a new paste of tobacco with a double dose of lime. He then lay down and tried to sleep a little. Yes, he thought as he dozed, that's how it had been, but perhaps Sanabria interpreted events in a drastic way. He meditated while gazing at the twin porcelain cups. Sanabria was like a brother, even though he was more humble and thoughtful than himself. It was better that way. He knew Sanabria would never let him down. Even if he rejected and disliked his impulsive improvisations, he would never let him down. Besides, he had been spared from many battles only because Sanabria had risked and sacrificed himself for his sake.

The three bayonet wounds at Acajutla were meant for him, but Sanabria had let them pierce the soft tree of his magnificent lungs. Moreover, Sanabria had requested a short song after the bomb attack at his birthday celebration. Sanabria looked after stool pigeons and took confessions from informers. Sanabria deposited bags of cash into his personal bank account in Miami. Without him power would be more lonely, even though less shared.

His *compadre* had gotten deeply under his skin. The only problem was that they desired the same material things. If only Sanabria could free himself from ambition, from worldly appetites, he would become immune and purified forever from human temptation, like the glorious Greek gods. The general imagined himself sinking into a spongy column of drowsiness where all his pains and memories were eased.

An hour later he was awakened by the distant sounds of gunfire. "The game begins," he said to himself and got up, relieved from his burdens and complaints. He emerged tranquil and with a heart like ice, impervious to triumph or disenchantment. All the fibers of his being formed a skein of pure will. Outside was the confusion of voices and officers firing orders for battle. He smiled at hearing a horse neigh. Sanabria would be arriving with the powerful army that would put down the guerrillas forever. He walked to the tent's entrance and pushed aside the mosquito net. A flood of morning light smelling of the sun adhered to his inflamed cheek, to the white fire of his temples, to his hands, to the circumference of his body, and enveloped him in luminous flashes that blinded him and made him grow old. Over the esplanade of the encampment, nearer than the three reddish cannons that now aimed at the mountain range, the new recruits practiced their acquired skills for battle. But the general thought he was the victim of dream's deception, the instrument of the juggling of time, a toy of the mirrors of thought. He saw the old dragging themselves, suffocating in their oily tatters, and dying in the stifling heat. He saw women lifting heavy iron and lead rifles, children, adolescents, invalids, and the sick in distorted formation carrying empty shells in their coffinlike boxes. He saw hands calloused from working the hoe sharpening spears and polishing bayonets. And for the first time he saw the light imprint a bare foot leaves in the dust. Behind this conscripted mob, the soldiers followed, heckling and threatening with their weapons, their faces like stray dogs. Colonel Sanabria rode among them like the angel of God.

And then the general discreetly summoned three veteran officers to his tent and communicated his order sharply, like an inevitable bolt of lightning: "Execute my *compadre,*" he said. The officers were stunned by this disconcerting enigma. Powerless, they saw the president cross over beyond the sea of compassion. They left, dumbfounded, to carry out the order.

When the gunfire exploded, General Fernández stood overwhelmed, gazing at the translucent walls of his chamber. "*Compadre*," he lamented, exhausted, as if he were talking to the dead man, "we believe what we want to believe, but realities impose themselves." He began to rummage through the dockets of treaties and folders of decrees. At last he found the official regulations for decorations given posthumously to heroes who had fallen in battle under the clawing rays of the sun.

HEAVEN'S SURGEON

Rogelio Sinán

Translated by Stephen Kessler

> A ruby are your lips,
> a jewel split in two,
> out of the crown of God
> taken just for you.
> —Becquer, *Rimas*

"You're back?" said the angel.

"I'm back," confessed the jeweler.

"I assume you haven't come to us this time as a secret agent of Satan. Step this way! Are all your papers in order? Let's see.... A *J* on your passport. Are you a Jew? Don't forget, we discriminate here. Everyone in his place, no joking around. Missing your vaccination? No, here it is. Okay, abstinence against eleven thousand temptations ... complete list of mortal sins ... soul search ... curial transit visa ... mercy quota.... Everything in order. All right! Your turn will come pretty soon, but careful! If you try to put anything over on us, into the boiler you go. Don't you forget, I've got big wings."

The other shrugged his shoulders indifferently. He wasn't even paying attention. Not wanting to prolong the interview, he distracted himself looking at some clouds where, in a mystical flight of jet propulsion, new souls were arriving.

"Go on in," said the angel. "Now you can settle accounts with old Saint Peter."

Slowly and silently, as if by magic, the ethereal gates opened.

The jeweler went into the lobby, looked around and, feeling himself watched by all eyes, sat down in the only vacant seat.

As in the reception room of a ministry or clinic, the souls were waiting their turn, shy and frightened, clenching their proper papers and "curricula vitae" in their hands. They had to present the documents to the venerable Saint Peter, Heaven's Doorman, whose stern visage and long white beard could be seen through a screen covered with signs and posters. "Visit Paradise." "No Vacancy." "Try Angel Wafers—The Best." "Do Not Enter." "See God's Effigy in Technicolor." "No Smoking." "Beware of Dog." "No Dogs Allowed." "Fly Empyrean Express." "Supersonic Clouds and Comforts." "Smile." "Wait Your Turn."

A neophyte angel asked the one at the gate: "How come you were so tough on the soul of that young jeweler? Was he here before?"

"Yes," said the other, "he came a little while back, not like now, but alive. You can imagine what he was up to! I won't even tell you. A crafty little devil trying to sneak in here like Cellini himself, Lord have mercy! It had been ages already since live people were allowed in heaven. Sure, they tried, because they're all mixed up and it's hard to make yourself understood with them. The time Dante came, what a mess! He had everything backwards. Even a little Beatrice... I'd better shut up. It was useless attending to that poet in the finest 'stil nuovo,' because then he went and wrote pure blasphemies and even said that in hell everyone goes around naked and that men and women are constantly carrying on. Better he shouldn't get into heaven and start stirring things up."

"But what about the jeweler?"

"You'll see.... The poor guy was totally devoted to his art back in Florence.... He was a disciple of the magician Benvenuto and, like him, did the most gorgeous work in jewelry. Fame brought him riches and adventures with courtesans; but he was in love with his art and got caught in the snares of a flirty, cerebral model. She was thin, fine, with sky blue eyes and silvery hair, the ideal type of beauty for his work, since he had to make a statue of Amphitrite for a fountain. You know who she is? The pale green goddess of the sea.

"Stark naked (get thee behind me, Satan!), the model loved to watch the passionate goldsmith who adored her, but she was cold, bloodless.

"'I wasn't meant for human love,' she said, 'My icy lips are not for kissing.'

"Little by little, the statue took shape from his skilled fingers. It was Amphitrite, with traces of woman, waves, and fish!

"In the leisure moments his creative fever allowed, he tried to find a way to bring her to life with his best kisses, but it was all in vain.

"'Your lips are frozen like a statue's,' he said to her, 'and kissing you I feel the cold of death.'

"Frightened, she covered herself (like Diana surprised in her bath) and whispered, smiling:

"'Don't confuse what's real with what's fictitious. Your anguish is intellectual. If you think about it, you'll realize that you don't desire me as a woman but as something abstract, fleeting, unattainable. What you love in me is Amphitrite. And she's what I seem to be, not what I am. And yet, just by seeming to be, I exist for you as the feminine form of the sea. Don't forget that the souls of goddesses and even their bodies taste of marble. If you want me human, give me other lips, since you're such a fine jeweler. What good is my beauty if I only inspire art and not men's love?'

"The sea-green Amphitrite insisted so much, that the goldsmith started going to visit astrologers, alchemists, and magicians. No one could help him.

"However, he didn't give up. He called on Satan.

"'Come on,' said Satan, rising from the depths, 'I'll let you into heaven. If you follow my instructions, you'll be able to steal the secret of life's creation from God.'

"Under Satan's direction, the goldsmith tricked Saint Peter with who knows what kind of lies, and managed to convince him that he'd make a statue of the Lord at rest, impossible of course because God never sleeps. At least that's what Christian doctrine says, which has me... Okay... You know that the Doorman always unveils the statues in heaven. Well, he took the bait out of pure vanity, because the secret is that when nobody's looking, God does take his little naps. But there's the lie, there's the trick! Our goldsmith knew the secret, knew how to sit tight, and as soon as he caught the Lord snoring, he switched a commercially worthless stone for one of the rubies in God's crown.

"Back in his studio, just as Lucifer had arranged it, Amphitrite was waiting naked, just lying around. It was almost midnight. The goldsmith had to act fast. He took the divine ruby, made a precise cut with his chisel, the gem split in two, and the deed was done.

"Satan said to him:

"'You'll notice something like a rip in your chest, but don't let that scare you. Follow my instructions.'

"In fact, he felt a tearing in his guts, but he made a tremendous effort of will. Then he saw something that shook him with fear. In his hand, the two red pieces of the ruby, bleeding, were squirming and wiggling like a couple of worms. Overcoming his anguish, he placed them against the mouth of the sleeping woman, and suddenly they became two deep red lips like a fleshy rose.

"Oh, but now the goldsmith couldn't kiss them. All his vital sap was crystallizing in a marvelous new ruby whose blood was forming, drop by drop, in God's crown.

"Amphitrite woke up transformed. In her warm and fleshy lips she felt the stirrings of vice and lust.

"She looked in the mirror. Was that her mouth speaking of love? No, behind her someone was begging for mercy. Who was that lying there dying, wounded by chance on the cold pavement? But passion's time is brief and pleasure never waits. How could she stop and talk with death when a fierce new life was roaring in her veins?

"She couldn't stop. Her lips dragged her away.

"And she disappeared into the night."

Old Peter pronounced the sentence: "You'll go back to earth to atone for your sin. Your soul will reincarnate in a young doctor. You'll live in an era very different from your own. Times have changed, centuries have passed. You'll notice strange things; styles, weapons, ideas, everything will seem muddled, everything changing fast. Men have grown weary of the world. Even beauty has died. Now only the joy of death exists."

A thousand strange and curious persons (photographers, journalists, and actors among them) are milling around in the hospital.

"Hello? Yes? What? The new doctor? I don't know. Wait a minute. . . .

Yes, he's here. No, this is another one. He just got here two minutes ago. All right!... He's coming. How's that? In the operating room? Okay!"

The desk nurse sets down the receiver and walks over to a little man who's sitting there, shy as an angel, wearing huge glasses and carrying a very funny-looking bag.

"Doctor! Yes, you! Didn't you say you're the specialist? Well, look, you fell out of the sky just in time. It's an emergency! Yes, hurry up! No, first go into the sterilizing room. What? You don't understand? Where do you come from?"

The young doctor, with his white smock and cap, enters the big operating room.

Laid out on the table, the patient is waiting, anesthetized. It's a movie star. Super famous. She's won three prizes—at Cannes, Mar del Plata, and Venice. She was getting ready to shoot *Lust*, a great neorealist film, when the accident happened. Fortunately, it's just a light scratch across the lips, but those two infected blisters, what a horror! The film is held up and a transplant has to be made—anything to save her lips. The truth of the matter is that the artist wants her mouth to be more in tune with what still has to be filmed.

The young doctor feels, calculates, measures; he goes down to the morgue, examines different cadavers; he observes among them the ones that give the fullest idea of lust and finally finds one made to order. It's a young woman with platinum blond hair whose lips, even though she's dead, are still red and even fleshy. By what strange mystery has that mouth kept its color?

He looks at the dead woman awhile and suddenly exclaims:

"It's Amphitrite!"

"No," says the male nurse. "It's Galicia. Everybody in the night life knows her. She was just in an accident and died a minute ago."

The young doctor studies the fine body; naked like this she looks like a statue, and something in his subconscious makes him exclaim again:

"Yes, Amphitrite, Amphitrite!"

Quickly, he cuts the thick lips. They seem to be bleeding; but no. They were red with a thick coat of lipstick. Nevertheless (and despite his gloves), he thinks he feels in his fingers something sticky and alive like a couple of worms.

The operation accomplished and the lips transplanted to the actress, the young doctor feels satisfied. He's sure that the new lips will give the heroine the expression she needs for her character's lusty role. Her mouth, now blooming like a flower of sin, will awaken in the public a thousand lascivious dreams. It's so convincing, even the director and the screenwriter are turned on. These two are so euphoric they can already hear the cash registers ringing. Now there's no doubt that *Lust* will be a smash at the box office, especially if it's marketed with the magic warning: "No One Under 18 Admitted."

A few days later, when it was announced that the star's bandages were to be removed, the hospital was swarming with journalists, photographers, famous actors and actresses. Everyone wanted to be there to witness the surgical wonder.

No one was allowed in the room, but the hallway was full of people. Expectation blazed in every face. Several of the actresses looked upset. A wave of jealousy swept over them; their voices were loud and tinged with bitterness.

Only the doctor, the makeup expert, and the famous fashion designer were with the star in her room.

Finally, a nurse gave the sign for people to enter. Everyone rushed in, astounded by the miracle.

"But what's this?"

"How can that be?"

"It's impossible!"

The star was smiling with lips more chaste and beatific than a nun's with the aura of sanctity.

The director and the screenwriter were distraught, while several actresses, jealous before, couldn't hide their laughter.

The transplanted lips had nothing to do with the passion and fire that had burned before on the star's mouth. Now they were pale lips, cold and dead like a statue's. They gave a certain impression of something faded, of skin drawn tight, and there was something sarcastic in her smile.

There was nothing to be done. The star herself didn't want to see anyone, she wanted to be alone. Soon she retired from the movies and even from the world, convinced that everything was a lie and that life was nothing but vanity, misery, boredom. Her death, serene, was celebrated by the Church with holy indulgences. It's even said that she was canonized.

"You're back?" said the angel.

"I'm back," affirmed the jeweler.

And as the gates were opened, one could hear a chorus of voices and a joyous sounding of trumpets. "Hosanna! Hosanna! Excelsis!" sang the angels. And the booming voice of God spoke out:

"Greet the highest surgeon of heaven!"

"What? Isn't that the jeweler who was reincarnated as a young doctor?" asked the neophyte angel. "Why all the honors?"

And the angel at the gate answered:

"It's the judgment of the Lord our God. The young doctor conquered sin."

"How so?"

"He invented plastic surgery!"

CLAMOR OF INNOCENCE

Lizandro Chávez Alfaro

Translated by Dan Bellm

Toward the end of the trip, after we had crossed the bay under several downpours and the glare of the sun was drying the moisture from his sombrero, Don Abelino said that all this would be changing soon, unless the devil himself pulled some impossible Axis counteroffensive out of his hat.

In spite of my adolescent confusion, I understood that "all this" meant these miserable six-hour crossings: half a day of slow sailing exposed to the elements, reduced to the austerity of a weather-beaten rowboat, the entire weight of our sluggish motion pressing on our very bones.

His fervor and concentration made it unmistakably clear which approaching change he meant: he was referring to the imminent victory of the Allies, who were pleasurably occupied just then with the demolition of Munich and Cologne.

What I still couldn't grasp was what connection could bridge the distance between those victories and this grim advance into a headwind toward his little dominion of swampland.

Innocently figuring, I tried to make out the hidden common denominator of these two terms and me, or of these two terms and him; the only thing I got was a feeling of stupidity, a feeling that everything was fragile.

I saw the shore approaching, brimming with green, with no borderline between water and vegetation; the overhanging branches touching the waves presented a façade that looked impenetrable. In back of me, past the man who worked the oar, the humidity blurred the contours of the jutting rocks, and the opposite shore was lead grey and spattered with white at the furthermost point where the harbor lay.

From the prow came the faint odor of tobacco in Don Abelino's pipe, which he had put out and relit a hundred times. He was calmly anchored in another of those withdrawn moods that separated his orders or his rare outbreaks of enthusiasm, always expressed with only a marginal interest in receiving an answer, much less in making himself understood. Up to that time he had granted me placid glances and wandering talk, both subject to his strict rule of concealing affection. I had granted him my involuntary imitation and an ever-sincere expectancy for his breaks in the silence: a kind of distant watchfulness.

We were entering the channel: a narrow waterway of little depth, hacked out of the mangrove swamp, which lay between a creek and the supposedly solid ground. All the work of men with axes, machetes, and shovels kept getting lost in the renovations imposed there by time; the shores were filled with crayfish, the water with toadfish, which raised little clouds of mud as they fluttered away. It was a winding strait, still subdued by the pride of a natural order that bore no relation to machines. The stability of this primitive, contemptuous indifference was shaken somewhat when Don Abelino, his voice resonating through the swamp, proclaimed his scheme of widening the channel so that in the abundant postwar era an amphibious boat could sail in and out.

I kept staring at the muck on the shore through which crayfish had bored, but Don Abelino's compelling scheme forced me to recall quickly what few facts I had gathered thus far about amphibious boats: they had a propeller and tires, a rudder and a steering wheel, an anchor and brakes, a keel and a chassis—to which I added the roar of its motor, penetrating the swamp like an announcement that even our little backwater would be visited by Victory.

At the landing I stayed behind to pet all the dogs on the property while he went off across the level, hard-packed sand, a knot of insects whirling around his head. The main house was built on stakes, narrow, mold-covered posts, which aimed to save it not only from the water but from the swarms of gnats. From its elevated corridors I could see the cattle grazing in complete accord with this semiaquatic life, the horizon of palm trees growing in floodwaters, and the overwhelming image of the mechanical prodigy rolling around, sailing, unstoppable; land and water mastered by a single invention, something heretofore found only in foreign lands, the protagonist of remote troop landings and patrol operations. Transposed from news reports, where I had seen it fixed on black and white paper, to that plane of existence corresponding to the rhythm of my breath, the amphibian reached its state of perfection, if not its absolute reality. As I imagined it hurling jets of mud and water into the air before or below me, it left the realm of possibility to become something necessary, inevitable. The scattered events of war found their precise form; until then I had understood them only as the vague repercussions of a clash of numbers—30 divisions, say, against 27,400 prisoners or dead. El Alamein, Saint-Lo, Guadalcanal, Stalingrad—the geography of fantasy was transfigured, trembling under a soundless explosion. Don Abelino called out to me from his room. Sitting in an armchair, he paused from reading his magazine, *On Guard*. With the same hand that slipped his bifocals onto the bridge of his nose, he indicated the pile of loose papers I ought to read and contemplate—thereby participating in the devotion and painstaking care with which he had separated them with a razor blade and perhaps even arranged them in order of presentation.

I withdrew to a corner where I could better immerse myself in the collection of articles and prints, sensing that beneath his cold offering he was proposing to share something that I was now in line to inherit. I learned that he had been following the amphibian since it had first appeared, that with these clippings I was receiving the illustrated history of a dream: conceived in the esoteric regions of eternity, definitively passed on through a compilation of fragments, preserved in material form for this album dedicated to a heroic kinsman. Restrained by our unspoken rule against getting carried away by emotion, we read separately, at the distance demanded by habit, but holding out new lines of contact on behalf of the amphibian, viewed here from every angle, described in each of its capacities—above all, so full of promise, like one betrothed. The anticipated re-uses of so much war materiel included flamethrowers for fighting plagues of insects, engines of every class of horsepower, hangars convertible to silos or stables, parachute cloth available for anyone who would still want to travel by sailboat, and sparklers for Christmas celebrations.

But out of this splendid inventory, we coveted only this one vehicle made to order for our swampy coastal terrain. Without taking out the pipe wedged between his loose, yellowed teeth, he asked me what I thought about all this; yes, I said, we would have to wait for the final stroke of victory, and then there would be public auctions in some marketplace of the victorious world.

It had been Don Abelino's custom to maintain the solitude of his walks around the estate. Laconic, rigid, he would rebuff any suggestions of companionship and suggest instead that I could more fittingly befriend the swamps roundabout. Quite studious in my lonely apprenticeship, I would improvise spears and fishhooks, watching him askance as he went off in his cowhide gaiters with his machete in a sheath, riding on a sluggish horse as he skillfully skirted the quagmires. Yet during this vacation—perhaps believing that I was showing acceptable signs of growth, or thinking that we were now fellow communicants partaking of a common desire—we went out together almost daily to fulfill our uncertain task of invoking the future. We scattered phrases into air exposed to abrupt occupations of sun and rain: the DUKW now showing advantages over the LVT in dense brush; the tires of one versus the spiked treads of the other; how the former had performed in Isigny and the latter in Guadalcanal. We speculated about geological similarities between Luzon and the muck on which we stood, sometimes with water up to our chests. When there remained no other task to ascribe to our pacified amphibian, we would lapse into silence like addicts sunken in vice, although each of us would continue polishing his part of the hallucination.

Shortly before my vacation ended we returned to the port town. Berlin had fallen. The ceremony for the opening of the school year included a solemn expression of celebration. On the stage of the auditorium a board was set up with a brief column of numbers, corresponding to the hymns we would sing in praise. Five hundred lowered heads with eyes closed, we gave thanks for the heavenly designs invoked in the minister's prayer. Then the enormous structure of mortised wood revealed its fine acoustical properties. The glass in the open windows rattled at the choir's mercy: deep voices, frail voices, my own voice stubborn, propelled by the force of simplicity, proud to be setting out over the bay in company with this multitude, to spread over its stagnant waters another surge of words poured out in solidarity. And my heart shook with joy, certain that the words sung mattered less than to participate without holding back. We sang and sang again, grasping our red-covered hymnals; I, immersed in this opportunity to exceed my bounds.

The resonance of good fortune gave way to the voice of our principal, a woman walled in by her aggressive but feeble manner. Probably anything would have appeared clumsy to me after our flights of song, but it was her chubby pink legs that offended me most, quivering from repressed vehemence in the center of the stage. I barely managed to hear her rambling remarks about the meaning of victory; the last echoes of my musical reverie left me only when she announced an upcoming public ceremony, a student assembly to which we were all to bring a fold-up wooden V, something built with care, with an eye for beauty and for the good name of our school. She stipulated the size, but as for the method, each of us would be free to produce it according to his own imagination.

Don Abelino found me sandpapering a pair of rulers which were decorated with a clover design at one end. He rewarded me with that smile of his that always left me wondering which state of calm he was in—tolerant or treacherous. I placed a circle of white enamel in the center of each clover and added a blue stripe going the length of each ruler and outlining the clover shape. The final varnish brought out the mahogany's blood-red color. A screw joining the two rulers at the base created the folding V: it was something stirring and brilliant, my homage to the sign of victory but in some veiled way also an allusion to the amphibious boat.

On the appointed day I arrived at school in my starched uniform with the V placed between the shirt and the waistband, whether to take away some of its solemnity or from sloth or plain shyness. Perhaps it was the latter feeling that hinted to me that there was something ostentatious and vaguely servile in all the pomp and circumstance of this kind of mass meeting.

We marched to the park, nearly flayed alive under the midmorning sun. There the entire student body of the town was formed into columns, converging on the spot that the authorities (collaborating with the trees that dominated the other half of the park) had declared to be the front of the bandstand, supplied for the occasion with a microphone and loudspeakers. First the vendors of fruit drinks and ices passed through, shielded from the sun by steaming sombreros, shoving their pushcarts among the parched columns of people and hawking their wares discreetly, with lowered voices. Next came the speakers; they too were shaded under the Victorian bandstand. And there I was, waiting for the opulent presentation of our many V signs, raised up with one unanimous cry, displayed in a single gesture which—minimizing our own sacrifice under the sun—would usher in the powerful reality of a new era soon to begin with the auctioning-off of war surplus. At the end of her long peroration, the decrepit voice of an old Englishwoman exerted itself to cry out "God save the Queen," and some of us thought that this might be the signal. I hastened to raise up my unfolded V. To my right I saw another V made with drum-sticks; up ahead, another made from ornately carved boards: three blundering V's held up against the heavy sun.

One August we heard the news from Japan. Hiroshima had been pulverized by a single weapon. The atomic bomb. The entire city. Not a single part of it spared. Hiroshima. I heard about it during the break between two classes. "They blew the whole thing up with one shot," said a classmate of mine, the gold fillings in his thick set of teeth sparkling with a drool of satisfaction. The explosion kept reverberating in that far-off, inconceivably dead land, but for me it was a nameless feeling that gnawed inside, amounting to a premonition of the end of the world, which would render useless even my yearning for the amphibious boat. But such a sudden leap landed me in an unfamiliar fog, and I would immediately seize once more upon the blissful expectation of new things to come.

I lived in constant vigilance, facing out to sea, facing the river; then again, the cargoes might arrive by air, consigned to some customs agent who would open his storeroom to the delights of a public auction. My nights were charmed by the far-off rumblings of an incoming vessel, the foghorn's gruff signal once more forcing me to imagine what pristine cargo the ship's tonnage might be carrying stowed deep to its very waterline. I examined Don Abelino's reading matter, certain that in his mute dedication to reading hovered the key which I would one day fish out between the lines. Walking along the banks of the port town, I wanted to sound the depth of the change I felt. Cautiously, I began to notice the gradual disappearance of the wartime boom: half-deserted wharves and warehouses, vacant waters that were once the landing place of barges equipped with massive outboard motors, their metal hulls painted yellow, the red and green glass of their lanterns, their stowage black with great clumps of rubber—a pure memory scattered across layers of purple clouds as evening fell.

The frustration that follows from mockery survived my capacity to forget. With boundless self-pity I played the destitute child who is fully prepared to perish except that he has a grand idea of being some titanic child-god, bestower of all favors save those lost in the mazes of oblivion.

The following year I was once more in Don Abelino's care during the months when the sun shines fourteen hours a day, when the marshes dry up and their dry beds crack but still retain enough underground moisture for planting rice. One afternoon he invited me to accompany him in burning a vast palm grove that was roasting from exposure to the sun. Sharing silence, we went off at an easy pace to determine the wind's direction; positioning ourselves at one end of the grove, we made torches from little *yolillo* palms; starting from a single match we ran in opposite directions, tossing flames into the overgrown foliage until we had kindled a wall of fire half a kilometer long; panting, we met up again further out. By that time the blaze was well along but contained, creating an immense howling composed equally of crackling branches and the calling of animals, of male to female caught in midcopulation, of herd to herd fleeing at a slower pace than the great chain of fire, of terror to terror as the scorching heat crept forward, flying, fed from one moment to the next by the dry brush and the fuel of fruits and leaves—a vast profile outlined here by monkeys singed in the impossible, fleeting act of leaping into the sky, there by vipers holding themselves upright on the utmost branch with the utmost vertebra: superimposed onto air that was also fire.

We sat on a fallen trunk for hours, taking in the howling and the stinking smoke. I broke the fervor of this undisturbed pose of rapt contemplation by venturing to ask what would become of the amphibious boat. In answer, Don Abelino flashed me the vertical lines of a constricted frown: blunt knife edges, frozen even in the midst of fire.

Years later—years well acquainted with genuine separations, excuses, strained relations, occasional letters exchanged across the distance of several countries—I came upon a news report about the battle of Inchon, the Korean War's masterpiece, in which fifteen hundred amphibious boats had formed the core of a coastal invasion. I clipped it carefully and sent it to him, as from a son to a credulous parent, not needing to add a letter of my own for him to catch the allusion to this new opportunity for hope: the amphibious boat might yet be auctioned off somewhere within reach of his yearning. In return I received in the mail an elongated parcel which likewise contained no letter, nothing more than the V with the clover design, as from a father to an insolent son, enough for me to hear his laconic, cutting voice telling me: You too were once a believer, *carajito*. Little fool.

KATOK

Delfina Collado

Translated by Kathleen Weaver

Nobody knew how it began...

The ancient Indian land extended its fortresses the whole length of the valley, under beaming cacao fields, soaring yellow bees, and the high blaze of open ears of corn. There the beat of drums—*tambores* and *tamboriles*—was the echo of pain, joy, and death; of peace or war.

Contributing to the ornate aspect of the settlement were treasures from the nearby mines of Talamanca, its sands shot through with gold ore, where goldsmiths wrought exquisite figurines, though most people tilled the land. Toilers of the moist, fertile earth with the blessing of the gods of water and vegetation.

Work, love, and hope grew in the translucence of the air, in the turquoise of the sky, in the fecundity of the soil.

On the days of great ceremonies dedicated to the God of Rain and

Sun Rays, canoes—loaded with an abundance of blossoming maidens, woven baskets, clouds, songs, and vessel gourds—glided out from the lake's shore.

The women brought earthen jars of *chicha;* the men, smoking tobacco from elaborately carved stalks of cane, wove palm-leaf skirts and flower garlands for the dancers. They played clay flutes, and on the trunks of avocado trees they inscribed songs, whose stanzas slipped away into the air's tranquility.

They danced and sang while they burned incense to their plumed gods and to their drowsing sorcerers, always by the shore of that emerald lake, full of secrets and interwoven with fragrances.

It was a peaceable life with flowers, tobacco, and song.

And Katok, the young and generous chief, he who had offered up his heart to the sun, governed over them. The air was sweet with mint, *pejivalle,* thyme, and lemon. *Tun-tun-tun,* the drums.

Nobody knew how it began...

That year the signs and portents started: first the fiery comet that appeared in the sky and that everyone contemplated in horror. Later, turbulent water seethed in the middle of the lake. Then blue flies inundated the region, and the *kotjka* trilled their augury of death.

Early one morning, under an amaranth moon, drummer-birds, flying over the vast area, again foretold misfortunes, with a shriek of devilish laughter.

At the same time, word came of the arrival of the invaders; Indian messengers came racing with the news: men with corn-colored hair were approaching in enormous ships.

Chief Katok thought:

"The season is in flower, with beaming ears of corn and the death-sound of the drum. The foreigners who must come are arriving.

"They differ from us in face and dress, in their sky-thunderings, and because they sit astride powerful animals with silver feet that cast off dazzling sparks."

Anguish was born in the heart of the chief; his soul turned to shadow.

The messengers spoke: "Those of the other race come on a footing of war. All the chiefs of these parts have battled them and been conquered."

Repeated death-rhythms came from the drum: *tun-tun-tun.*

Katok asked himself:

"Since the strangers seek and desire only gold and silver, we would do well to bring those bearded ones our treasures and spread them out until they cover the plain. Let them take these things and leave us in peace; let them return to their own hearths.

"Do I not trust more in my right and reason than in our arms and power?

"Ah, now the prophecies of our ancient fathers and grandfathers, handed down through generations, are fulfilled: our race and our gods will perish at the hands of a new race of men."

The tribe's Council of the Ancients was of the opinion that the encounter with the foreigners should be safeguarded by their own army, but the Indian chief refused.

Katok spoke:

"My sons and brothers, we shall go in peace; if we present ourselves in arms it will look as if we are going to wage war. We shall welcome them with abundant gifts, since that is what they seek and desire."

As he spoke, a feeling of profound melancholy invaded him. His heart felt great pain for the people who gave him birth, among whom he grew to manhood and had his home; for the people he loved.

Already cries of alarm were coming from the Indian lookouts by the wall of blue water. The plaints of the drums had turned to tears: *tun-tun-tun*.

Year of death and destruction.

Under a drizzling, gray sky the captain sent forth his group of emissaries, led by Fray Primero.

They plunged the Christian standard, blazoned with a cross, into the ground. The friar spoke: "I am the messenger of a king you must venerate and serve. You shall revere and love the cross and believe in the Gospel of Christ. You shall adore nothing else."

Katok replied:

"I adore only the undying sun, my burial grounds, and my gods, the mountain that gathers in the clouds and transforms them into precious crystalline water, which engenders everything that lives and nourishes us.

"In my realm I am a great lord; I know the ancient and forgotten things; I practice tradition; religion is my fortress and my reason for living.

"We who are native here do not covet gold or silver; we take only what we need to dream, not to live. Our bodies are like the springtime grasses that flower and wither away.

"Let the strangers return to their homes and we will give them treasures; we will offer them ears of corn, cacao, flowers, sweet, succulent fruits; we will give them feather adornments and embroidered shawls."

As he spoke he looked at them and thought: "What strange men, who cover their faces with moon-colored gourds adorned with bells and feather crests, which let only the eyes be seen.

"All dressed alike. Strange."

They brought thundering sticks and clothed horses. They had lost their judgment to riches and baptized his Indian land with the name of Costa Rica, a coast rich in legends and treasures.

He already knew that the captain and his soldiers had entered the neighboring territory and annihilated thousands of Indian warriors. Much blood had flowed. They killed Indians as if they were flies. They raped young girls and tore open the wombs of pregnant women.

Those they did not destroy they tortured to make them tell the whereabouts of their treasures. They took away their food and clothing. Later, their women and children.

They had no fear of the god they proclaimed. Nor was there justice.

Katok's heart suffered for his people. The drum repeated the rhythms of death: death-death-death.

Katok felt:

Free as the eagle, strong and intelligent as the puma, tremendous warrior. With his corn, his cacao, his nahual-spirit, his jaguar, and his magic herbs. Then he envisioned himself captive, bound and humiliated, severed at the root, his existence at an end, his domains usurped, his world razed to the ground. His copper-skinned tribe lost in wandering and slavery, like a dark flock. He saw them dying or living on in servitude. Perspiring blood. Perplexed, broken, disoriented, homeless. Only faces, millions of coppery faces, sweating sorrows, dispersed, empty-wombed.

Their guardian shadow dead. With no one to turn to, nowhere to go. Roaming without mountain or valley, leading a crushed, wandering life. *Tun-Katok-tun-tun.*

Fray Primero told Katok that the captain wanted an audience.

Katok decided to receive him in the plaza. He wore his royal insignia and finest garments, all interwoven with tiny gold plates, bells, and mosaics of shining feathers; he sat beneath a green-plumed canopy upon a high platform, attended with all honors, surrounded by priests and by the people.

The white men arrived, approached the plaza, closed off all entrances and exits, and fell upon the chief, stripping him of his royal insignia and jeweled garments.

With swords and harquebuses they murdered everyone else. Those men the color of dark earth were slaughtered like animals, slashed to pieces; their heads were severed and impaled on sticks; they were stabbed and ripped open, their entrails scattered. Indian blood flowed like water.

When all were dead, Katok was taken prisoner, flanked by soldiers and harquebuses. He was bound and placed in leather cords, his tawny body absolutely naked. He was tied with twisted leather and chained in irons. The white men tormented him:

There is no pom, no tune, no sun,
only the dry echo of the tun,
rhythm of death tun — tun

Katok spoke:

"Sovereign Christian, hard of heart and deaf of spirit. You destroy our gods and our past. You take away our lands and our heritage, our wives and our daughters.

"You are red like your beards. Red like the hot flame of your harquebus. Red as the wound of your crucified god, that god who permits you to desecrate and exterminate us. Red as the blood of the maidens you have outraged. Your hands are red with the blood of my children and my brothers and sisters. Yes, you walk the earth burning red with blood. You will pay beneath the sky and upon the earth. I will say no more to you. My mouth has no more words."

He looked at the fire that leapt with lascivious blue tongues to lick the air. A cricket uttered a drumlike moan upon the wooden arm of a cross. No more did Katok hear the delicate goldfinch voice of his woman, or the whisper of leaves that is the soul of the jungle, the river, and the corn.

Katok's eyes filled with blood. Mortal anguish in his soul. His heart fainted. Slid. He felt himself utterly light, utterly distant from his land now darkened and loosed from its moorings. Heaven or earth?

His mind was hallucinating, drifting. A subtle nimbus enveloped him; he soared over the corn, over the cacao fields, over thousands of orchards, over his adored mountain. Behind him cacophonous echos. He flew through space, boundless, into the infinite. Clouds enveloped him in aromas of white stars and bore him ever higher, higher, higher.

Nobody knew how it began... The palm trees, *jinocaubes*, and *jaules* swayed in distress. Leaves dropped from the willows. Gigantic ferns shriveled in jungle anguish. Gray and grieving, the wind drew in upon itself in sobs, then suddenly, spinning like a top, blew off down rows of cacao trees, carrying with it leaves, heron and quetzal feathers, wildflowers and dust, beating down the tropical orchids.

The jungle wept. In urgent concert rose the drums—the *bribis, huetares, cabecares, bruncas, terrebas*, then the *chorotegas*—all spread the news:

Tun — tun — tun
Katok is dead.
Tun.

The bonfires died out; twilight shadows faded; silence fled. Laments flooded the valley; the earth moaned; the jaguar roared; the fields sighed in mourning. The chorus of the drums' wounded parchments exploded on every breeze: *tun-tun-tun*. All the Indians asleep under rocks and soil, Indians of every age, felt Katok's death.

Tun — tuun — tuuun
Katok is dead,
deaad — deeaaad.

Dawn of a new day. Auroral light. Beaming sky. The orchids and everlastings are in bloom, drenched with light. The sedge plants lean to kiss the lake. When chief Katok entered the darkness of death, he was reborn with the dew. Reborn. Illumining the earth with his strong and powerful life, as seen by his people through his Death.

A new god: Katok. God of peace and love, he is born.

Katok — god — lives:
in rhythm — sun — pom and tun,
Katok — god — Katok.

WE BAD

Salarrué (Salazar Arrué)

Translated by Thomas Christensen

Goyo Cuestas and his youngster pulled up stakes and lit out for Honduras with the phonograph. The old man carried the works over his shoulder, the kid the bag of records and the beveled trumpet element, tooled like a monstrous tin-plated bellflower that gave off the fragrance of music.

"They say there's money in Honduras."

"Yeah, Dad, and they say they've never heard of phonos there."

"Get a move on, boy—you've been dogging it since we left Mepatán."

"It's just that this saddle's about worn my crotch raw!"

"That's enough—watch your tongue!"

They laid up for a nap under the whistling and aromatic pines. Over an ocote-wood fire they warmed up coffee. Rabbits huddled in an uneasy quiet in the *sapote* grove, browsing. Goyo and the boy were approaching the wild Chamelecón. Twice they saw traces of the *carretía* snake, thin as the track of a belt. When they stopped to rest, they put on a fox trot and ate tortillas with Santa Rosa cheese. For three days they made their way through mud up to their knees. The boy broke down crying; the old man cursed and laughed at him.

The priest in Santa Rosa had cautioned Goyo not to sleep in the shelters, because gangs of thieves constantly patrolled for travelers. So at nightfall Goyo and the boy went deep into the underbrush; they cleared a little spot at the foot of a tree and there they spent the night, listening to the singing of cicadas and the buzzing of blue-tailed mosquitoes as big as spiders, not daring to breathe hard, trembling with cold and fear.

"Dad, you seen *tamagases* snakes?"

"No, boy, I checked the trunk when we turned in, and there weren't any hollows."

"If you smoke, pull down your hat, Dad. If they see the embers they'll find us."

"OK, take it easy, man. Go to sleep."

"It's just I can't sleep all bunched up."

"Stretch out, then...."

"I can't, Dad, it's freezing."

"The devil with you!... Curl up against me then!..."

And Goyo Cuestas, who had never in his life hugged his son, took him against his foul skin, hard as a rail, and, circling his arms around him, warmed him until he was sleeping on top of him, while he, his face twisted in resignation, waited for daybreak to be signaled by some far-off rooster.

The first daylight found them there, half frozen, aching, worn out with fatigue, with ugly mouths open and driveling, half folded up in their ragged blankets, dirty, and striped like zebras.

But Honduras is deep in the Chamelecón. Honduras is deep in the silence of its rough, cruel mountains; Honduras is deep in the mystery of its terrible snakes, wildcats, insects, men.... Human law does not reach to the Chamelecón; justice does not extend that far. In that region, as in primitive times, it is up to men to be good- or bad-hearted, to be cruel or magnanimous, to kill or to spare according to their own free will. Clearly the right belongs to the strong.

The four bandits entered through the fence and then settled in the little square of their camp, that camp stranded like a shipwreck in the wild cane plantation. They put the phonograph works between them and tried to connect the trumpet element. The full moon made flashes of silver appear on the apparatus. From a beam of their lean-to hung a piece of stinking venison.

"I tell you it's a phonograph."

"You seen how it works?"

"Yeah!... In the banana plantations I seen it."

"Youdunnit!"

The trumpet worked. The highwaymen cranked it up and then opened the bag of records and lifted them to the moonlight like so many other black moons.

The bandits laughed, like children from an alien planet. Their peasant clothes were stained with something that looked like mud and that was blood. In the nearby gully, Goyo and his youngster fled bit by bit in the beaks of vultures; armadillos had multiplied their wounds. Within a mass of sand, blood, clothing, and silence, their illusions, dragged there from far away, remained only as fertilizer, perhaps for a willow, perhaps for a pine....

The needle touched down, and the song flew forth on the tepid breeze like something enchanted. The coconut groves stilled their palm trees and listened in the distance. The large morning star seemed to swell and shrink, as if, suspended from a line, it was moistening itself by dipping into the still waters of the night.

A man played the guitar and sang a sorrowful song in a clear voice. It had a tearful accent, a longing for love and glory. The lower strings moaned, sighed with desire, while the lead strings hopelessly lamented an injustice.

When the phonograph stopped, the four cutthroats looked at one another. They sighed....

One of them took off, sobbing into his poncho. Another bit his lip. The oldest looked down at the barren ground, where his shadow served as his seat, and, after thinking hard, he said:

"We bad."

And the thieves of things and of lives cried, like children from an alien planet.

THE GUAYACAN TREE

Bertalicia Peralta

Translated by Dan Bellm

The night was steaming, and the air coming in through the openings in the walls was hot, and the blood of the people who lived in the town was hot.

Dorinda couldn't sleep. She was thinking, not dreaming. Sometimes she dreamed about sweet and beautiful things she had never had. But now she wasn't dreaming or sleeping, just thinking, and her thoughts were like vine branches twisting around in her mind, crushing her brain and making her dark almond eyes glaze over. She stirred on the rickety old bed. It was a slight movement, but even so the man beside her seemed to feel it because he curled up and tried to press closer to her. Dorinda shied away. She felt a boundless disgust for this hard, sweating body that had stayed on top of hers for so many years, above her, pressing on her breasts and thighs, panting over her stomach, tearing into her sex, always forcing her open, trying to destroy her. She moved to the opposite side of the bed.

"Let's go out dancing," he had said to her one day long go. She had just stood there looking at him. What was he after? "Let's go," he kept saying. But she didn't go. Who would take care of her three little babies at home? There were plenty of stories of unfit mothers leaving their infants at home alone while they went out to a dance, and then something terrible happening. Sorrow came upon them, sure enough: one mother's house burned down with the little ones locked inside, where she thought they would be safe; another time some brute had raped a little girl only five or six years old. No. She didn't go. She needed to take care of her children.

But other dances and other encounters came along, and he kept pursuing her. The suspicion she felt at first gave way to a kind of habit. She got used to having him around, even though there were plenty of things about him she couldn't stand. Like his habit of fighting with her children, who weren't his own, his resentful attitude when looking at them or talking to them, and eventually his deceitfulness, his way of pretending, even when he could see she knew the truth. It was like playing fox and hen. She could tell that he only wanted her, and to get her he was willing to trick her into thinking he liked the little brats. But she knew it wasn't so.

And then his drinking. Back when he was good he worked hard. He controlled himself. He even had his moments of kindness and tenderness, long looks that led to lovemaking in the woods, tumbles and frolics far from the house, pleasures under the cloudless sky. She liked him then—so much so that he moved in with her, and they lived together happily ever after. Dorinda laughed softly to herself. No. "Happily ever after" was how the stories they read to her in school always ended, years ago when she was a girl and her grandmother sent her to school up to second grade. Happy. Well, why deny it, they were a little bit happy sometimes, when he was making money, when they went to a dance and he embraced her gently—before getting drunk. That didn't last long. The more he drank the crazier he got, and he would squeeze her in his arms, but only so he wouldn't fall down, the fucking bum, and he kept an eye on her when other men were around, and then she would have to go home alone and wait for him to come in like an animal and throw himself on top of her and try to rape her, but with no enthusiasm or strength because he'd be so drunk he would sleep until noon the following day.

Dorinda got up and walked out of the house. It was cooler outside.

In March the earth was hot, the air was hot—even one's blood was hot. She drew some cool water from the earthen jar. The worst was when he started in about children. Now he wanted children—children of his own, since the others weren't his. She knew he hated them, especially her little girl. But she wasn't going to have any more children. She had asked all about it at the health center. The doctor had advised her and now she knew what she needed to do. Even though she had tried not to, she became pregnant again. She didn't say anything, but he caught on. Her belly began to stretch, her breasts filled up, her eyes became more sunken. He knew. And he told everybody. And he stayed drunk for a week.

"So, Dorinda, we're adding on to the family, eh?" people around town started saying.

"Don't believe everything you hear," she would answer.

"Well, what about this little tummy you're growing? I'd say you must be around the third month, aren't you?"

"Didn't you hear me? I'm not having any more children."

Dorinda took in the cool night air. The night was dark. Not a single star. A splendid blackness covered the whole earth. She pulled her hair up into a bun.

"Why did you go spreading this news around?" she asked the man. "I'm not having any more children—I'm going to rip it out of me." She said it calmly, decisively. The three children weren't at home. He was lying on the hammock, smoking. She was grinding corn, slowly, rhythmically, her stomach pressing the edge of the table. Her arms rose and fell with strength and confidence.

"Are you crazy?" he said. And before she knew it he threw himself on her, grabbed her by the shoulders, spun her around, and glared into her eyes like a wild animal.

"Are you crazy? You do that and I'll kill you. I'll kill you!" Then he ran out and got drunk again that night and told the whole world about it. For the first time Dorinda was afraid. He would do it. He was an animal—he'd do it. He was too stupid to realize how useless he was around the house. She worked all day and half the night; it didn't matter to him. All he would talk about was how they weren't his kids. And the boys were getting big; soon it would be time for them to go to school. They weren't going to grow up to be fools like they were. That was that. So she started to think about it. She calculated day and night, trying to add up the advantages of staying with him. She couldn't think of one. On the contrary, she had aged ten years in the two that had passed since that first night he set foot in her house.

Slowly Dorinda walked down to the stream, which was nearly dry from the summer heat. She did everything as they had told her. And the stream carried away the blood that flowed from her as she squatted and endured the pain.

Then she lay down on the grass to regain her strength. Tears streamed from her eyes, blinding her vision, burning her eyes as if salt had been poured into them. She wailed. She felt a pain so deep inside her—this pain had always been there, but she had never known it. She wept until she was free of it. She stood up and walked slowly back to the house.

The man was asleep. She had taken care of that, too; not even a fire would have awakened him. The children weren't at home. She had sent them to her sister's "so they could get to know their cousins a little better"—as if that were necessary in such a small town.

Dorinda drew closer to the bed. The man was sweating. She remembered the times he had sweated all over her, trying to rip out her insides. He could do without her. He had never really needed her at all, and she knew it. He was hardhearted. If he said he would kill her, he would. But she wouldn't let him. No. Not now. Dorinda wasn't going to let certain things happen to her anymore, even if no one knew that yet. She drew closer to the man. She pressed his skin, shook him, shoved him. He was dead to the world. But she knew he was alive—just fast asleep.

Calmly, she went into the kitchen. She got the knife and gripped its handle hard. She plunged it several times into the man's heart. The blood ran in torrents, gushing out at first, then more slowly until it stopped. So much blood; it reeked. She made sure that he was dead, but even so she drove the knife into his body three more times. The night was still black and hot. She closed the windows and lit a lamp, soft and low. She tried to move the dead man but realized he was too heavy for her alone. So she set to work and began to carve him up, bit by bit—first the head, then the arms and legs. When she had got it all into little pieces, she put the body in a henequen sack and fastened it with a slender reed. She dragged the sack out of the house, fetched her horse, and tied it to the cinch. Then she mounted the horse and dragged the henequen sack down to the pasture on the other side of the hill. When she got there her face was cool and unperturbed, her deep-set eyes as mysteriously bright as ever. She dug the deepest pit she could. Her body followed her mind's impulses; it was used to rough country work. She shoved the henequen sack inside and covered it with earth. She planted a guayacan tree and returned to the house.

The rest of the night she spent carefully scrubbing all the bloodstains away. The stench troubled her; it seemed to be ground into the dirt floor, into the walls and the bed.

Morning came clear and bright. Dorinda went down to the stream quite early to wash and found other women there.

"Well, Dorinda," said one of them, "how's the little baby?"

"Didn't I tell you that was nothing but gossip?" she answered. "There's no man around here to get *me* pregnant!"

"And what about Jacinto?" they asked, just to be asking something, just to be saying something while they pounded their washing on the stones.

"He left this morning," Dorinda said. "He said he was going to see if he could find work in the Canal Zone, and if he couldn't he'd jump ship for somewhere. Most likely he won't be back."

So Dorinda went down every day with her children to water the little sprig of guayacan. It was only March and she wanted it to grow tall and fill with blossoms.

A SURRENDER OF LOVE

Juan Aburto

Translated by Barbara Paschke

"I had a sweetheart once, but he was killed," the woman told me sadly, looking down at the floor as if she were talking to herself.

Still attractive, she was in her forties and unmarried.

"It was a long time ago, in the days of the elder Somoza. I was just a girl and he was older; he was very intelligent and the two of us were in school together; he was studying law and was almost finished with his degree. But we both got involved in the student protests. He organized, gave speeches, led strikes, and wrote newspaper articles against the dictatorship. Sometimes, during the protest marches, the National Guard came out and pursued us, striking out at us violently. We ran through the streets, scattered in all directions, and two or three blocks later rejoined the crowd, ending up with split heads and sore ribs, but we kept on with the speeches and leafletting. Right then the jeeps appeared and a few of the guard and again they broke up our group with blows and kicks. So we wouldn't lose each other in the uproar, my friend and I grabbed each other's hands and ran together through the tumult of people and soldiers. When we couldn't run any more and the streets were blocked, we ducked into a doorway at random, breathless and terrified. The people took us in, nursed our wounds, and hid us for a while. Then we continued on."

The woman spoke slowly and paused often. She looked pensive, as if recalling every detail of her past, reconstructing it step by step as if to relive it right now.

"Sometimes they shot to kill. Many fell. In the distance we could hear the roar of the Garands firing rounds and the pof, pof of the tear-gas bombs. The smoke surrounded and poisoned us; we could feel an intense heat entering through our noses and going into our brains and lungs and some people fainted. We couldn't keep from crying and then we started to vomit. Later on, we learned how to protect ourselves from tear gas by putting damp handkerchiefs over our noses and mouths. But the next day we were always out there again.

"He was taken prisoner several times. I went to see him in jail and they almost never let me go in because they said he was incommunicado. But when I could get in I brought him bread and cigarettes and sometimes a book to read. We spoke briefly, holding hands, separated by bars, with an armed guard next to us. We couldn't kiss because there was a thick railing that prevented us from getting close. But he told me that when he got out he'd go back to the university and soon he'd be a lawyer and then we'd get married and Nicaragua would be free. We squeezed our hands tightly and I cried a little, but from happiness, from hope, and, well, from all that joy... we were going to have... you know... him free and the two of us together and the country free, too.

"Months passed and I kept waiting for him. Since he wasn't around, I helped the other protest organizers. I put up posters, convinced students to incorporate themselves with other schools, carried or mailed messages to other parts of town. Because of all that, I wasn't studying much, but I liked what I was doing because it was his work and I also liked all the other people involved, and everyone—well, all good Nicaraguans—wanted a free country without tyranny.

"He finally got out but didn't stay free for long. When he went back to work in the same campaign, they arrested him again. And this time they even beat him. Since now they knew he was one of the student leaders, they persecuted him even more. And when they grabbed him another time, they kept him prisoner even longer and beat him more severely. He came out covered with marks, with scratches, scrapes, and bruises all over him. But he didn't care. Once again he returned to fighting for freedom, and he even talked to me once about going up to the mountains to join the guerrillas. I talked him out of it so that he would stay with me; I told him that here he could fight politically with his other student friends.

"But in no time they arrested him again. Now they didn't even wait to get him in the streets but went to look for him in his own house or wherever he was hiding. And they began to torture him every time they arrested him. They hung him up, made him drink salt water, and used electric prods on him. But they got nothing out of him! When he came out he was terribly thin and sickly but even more passionate.

"Of course he couldn't go back to the university. He was too well known and they gave orders that he wasn't to be admitted, and even though he wasn't doing anything, they arrested him again just as he was leaving a crowded popular spot, and again they thrashed him. We had no rest, or diversions either. Always struggling, working for freedom, or hiding."

The woman held back a sob and was quiet for a while, staring into space; then, giving a big sigh, she continued.

"Only once did we ever have a party. Some friends planned an outing to the river. We all went and took food and drink and guitars. There were more than fifteen of us in the group. We spent the whole day swimming, singing, and eating, and even making political plans.

"You know something? I went there with my sweetheart and we got even closer to each other. How can I explain it?"

The woman had become flustered and noticeably anxious, something between happy and sad. I didn't say anything so that she could get over her shyness and relax.

"It's just that there, well... it's not that anything bad happened, you know? It's just that it was like we had suddenly gotten married, among all the people there, you see? But there was no marriage, you know? How can I explain it?"

I really didn't understand anything, but I didn't ask for an explanation. "Uh huh?" I said nothing else. She laughed a little.

"It's just that it embarrasses me to talk about it!"

She laughed quietly. Smiling and blushing, she tilted her head as if she wanted to hide between her shoulders, and looked down.

"It's just that I don't know how to say it.... But, oh well, I'm going to tell you! It was like this: from that moment we were joined together, understand? But without anything legal. But for us it was true. Even though we didn't talk about it later. Nor did we say anything to the people who were there at the picnic with us.

"Anyway, the girls had hung up a sheet between two trees so we could take off our clothes and put on our bathing suits. Everyone was changing and going out to lie on the grassy bank with the boys and eat and drink and play guitar.

"I was the last one. I had taken my clothes off and was standing there with nothing on, moving my head from side to side looking for my bathing suit among all the clothes on the ground. I couldn't find it. Then I felt a shadow above me. I focused my attention and fearfully saw a man's head appearing above the sheet. Right away I recognized him. The same hair, the wide forehead, bushy eyebrows, the same black eyes. Uriel! I said. But I didn't move. He didn't either. He rose up a little and I could see more than half his face. He kept looking at me as if he were frightened, his eyes open wide. I felt like I was going to laugh, seeing him so shocked, but I stayed serious. I let him see me completely. I mean, he certainly had the right; he was my sweetheart. And I loved him. He loved me too, and we had already agreed we were going to get married.

"He took in all of me with his look, the thief.... But I let him. I didn't move a muscle. With that, I believe I totally surrendered myself to him. Even though nothing else happened. Not then, not later.

"He didn't touch me at all. But from that instant I felt I was no longer alone. I felt like now we were two, united. But I felt happy and content.

"And there he was, looking and looking at me. And there I was, immobile, letting him have that pleasure. After a while, he lowered his face behind the sheet. I felt strange. Like I had really been his during those brief moments, and now I was someone else. I must say I liked it. But I didn't say anything to anybody. Nor did I mention it to him later."

The woman sat thinking in silence, a melancholy expression on her face.

As for me, I imagined taking part in her story, like being in a play about an encounter with Pan, a vision of a satyr (I myself the satyr) in some hellenic forest.

The guanacastes are laurels, the sheet a thick wall of myrtle; along the side, the river's soothing drag, perhaps the crackling of some cicadas. And behind the myrtle, laughs, voices, and the sound of the nymph's lyre. It's summer and the warm breezes are blowing, vibrating from above. Meanwhile, a head with curly hair, two incipient horns, and a sensual, short, tangled beard surges above this sylvan setting. The eyes give off confused sparks, drilling into the other blue eyes and opening wide over the face, astonished, as if they had never seen the glowing face of a woman. And now they move down slowly: very white breasts, firm as marble; hair in a chestnut cascade intertwined with flowers, flowing over her shoulders; her stomach almost celestial, gathering the green shadow of the glade; brief and almost golden down wedged in the vertice of her virgin body; the sweetest legs with mother-of-pearl skin, tiny and slender feet disappearing into the moist rocky ground. The nymph, surprised with a vine in her hand, head held high, moves her arm slightly away from her body, as if granting entry, as if making her surrender of love definitive.

After a few moments of silence, the woman spoke again.

"Well, as you can imagine, a short time later the guard arrested him again. And that time it seemed like an eternity. They kicked him brutally, did barbaric things to him, and finally killed him. They told the family he had fallen from the bunk in his cell. But that was a lie. He was crushed inside. Completely black and blue with blood coming out his ears, his nose, his mouth, everywhere. They had beaten him to a pulp. That's how they handed him over, dead.

"Years later the revolution came to save us, to save the country. And now we're free here, we have new hope. I've been alone since then. And I'm resigned to it, even though he never saw any of this. I loved him, and they killed him. We never lived together, he never became a lawyer, we never married, nothing."

The woman was silent for a moment, then she gave a faint, bitter smile and said:

"But he saw me naked. . . ."

THE LAST FLIGHT OF THE SLY BIRD

Jorge Luis Oviedo

Translated by Steve Hellman

After many years of incessant labor he managed to complete his college degree.

The thought began to gnaw at him one morning after the professor read us something on a character in Greek mythology who flew using wings that he himself had made.

That same night Cesarín dreamed he flew over the town in front of astonished parents and friends, who applauded him with deafening enthusiasm. So it was that the following day he decided to do first things first, and he quit school in order to devote all his time to constructing a pair of wings; and being as he was the wise man of the family, his stepparents had no recourse other than to consent to his project and see it as a fit of insanity.

"It's God's will," said Clementina, satisfied with the reward of annoyance from her closest neighbors.

Almost two months later, Cesarín had finished building a pair of cardboard wings with the help of a harnessmaker and a carpenter. He contemplated them with a satisfaction that could not be contained in his face and a look that confirmed, by chance, that they were as enormous as his madness.

On Sunday the whole family rose at dawn, and when the day grew light, they set out for one of the properties of Juan José de Jesús Antonio de la Sierra. By the time the chiming bells announced six o'clock mass, they had already arrived at the peak. They saw the sun lift its head over the line of mountains and, like a powerful eastern king, insatiably drink the mists and the morning frost, while they proceeded to fasten the wings to Cesarín, who extended them with the clumsiness of a tired buzzard and, trying to find courage, exclaimed: "We'll make it, Mama, you'll see, we'll make it."

"Yes, tomorrow you'll be famous," she replied, with a restrained tone of doubt which she desperately tried to hide behind a bright smile that was outlined in her face with the delicacy of a bad portrait artist. She pictured Cesarín flying over the town and nearby villages, held up by a magic thread and appearing in all the country's newspapers, photographed in full flight, while the news spread throughout the world, referring to the amazing feat of her adopted son.

His stepfather, still skeptical, observed all the goings-on from the slope. He calculated the size of the drop as he gazed down into the ravine that opened at his feet like the womb of a woman postpartum; but when Cesarín was ready, he only thought to say, "God's will be done." Almost instantly he saw his stepson make the final lunge, arrive at the edge of the abyss, and attempt a useless flapping. Cesarín, for his part, didn't have time to think of anything while descending swiftly like a lifeless object into the ravine's throat.

When, two hours later, he was awakened by the tumult raised by the people his stepfather had contracted to rescue him from the branches of those trees that almost miraculously had interrupted his path to save him from certain death, the one thing that stuck in his mind was that it was only his first try.

Don Juan José de Jesús Antonio de la Sierra tried to dissuade Cesarín, telling him that when he completed his bachelor's degree, he would send him to the United States to study aviation, and that, as a graduation gift, he would buy him a small plane so that he could fly to his heart's content.

Everyone believed that given such an offer Cesarín would desist, but he hadn't even fully recovered from his multiple contusions when he again undertook a new project (not necessarily to be daring, as the reporters say). It didn't take long to construct a new pair of wings, this time with the help of an ingenious tailor and an accomplished carpenter, who constructed a set from bamboo frames and a cotton print. Although very similar in appearance to the previous ones, these looked light and resistant.

With the experience gained from his first failure, Cesarín preferred to wait a few weeks in order to exercise daily, the idea being to acquire the necessary strength by the time of his second effort. Almost a month later he invited his closest friends and relatives who, attracted by the extravaganza, kept the date. The results couldn't be more disastrous than those of the first attempt. Only this time he fell into a pool of incredulous bathers who took charge of rescuing him. Nearly everyone believed, according to what they confessed hours later, that he went down like a dying angel, but soon they discovered the irreplaceable face of Cesarín, which still reflected only the terrible and repressed desire to fly.

One dawn he awoke startled and leapt up with such joy that it spread to his younger brothers and finally to all the family and even to the nearest neighbors, who rose thinking there was a fire. The disturbance, however, was due to a brilliant idea (according to the adjective he had granted it). As always, his mother opted to humor him completely and interceded so that her husband would yield to Cesarín's plans. Thus it was that during the periods when the herons arrived to eat the ticks off the cattle of Don Juan José de Jesús Antonio de la Sierra, his workers dedicated themselves to killing the herons and plucking them clean, managing to collect in a short time a total of 2,266,729 feathers, a quantity more than sufficient to manufacture Cesarín's newest set of wings.

"They are more beautiful than angel's wings," Clementina said, full of joy, when she saw them finished.

From then on, no one doubted Cesarín's madness and how in two months it had clearly infected Clementina, who had completely abandoned her religious duties to follow her stepson's training in detail.

Her next-door neighbor, Azucena Martínez, very given to venturing opinions, said that Cesarín had more the sorcerer in him than the saint. Clementina, however, maintained that he was a product of God's will. The rest of the people, more attached to logic and reality, considered that everything was due to the collective madness that had infected the whole family, which is why they were very often heard to say: "No one is wise to whom it might occur to support such nonsense."

Finally, to end the attempts that threatened to become endless, his stepparents arranged a date and a place to bring about the last flight, in agreement with Don Juan José de Jesús Antonio de la Sierra, who had decided that if Cesarín didn't kill himself (which was most likely), he would in no way support Cesarín any longer. Because calling it the last flight was better than calling it the third try, people agreed in a casual and spontaneous way to call it "the last flight of the sly bird."

Therefore, notice spread to all the surrounding area, and on the third Sunday in May, 1968, at four in the afternoon, one hour before the flight, the town was packed. Everyone (even the reporters) roamed about looking for the best vantage point from which to watch every bit of the spectacle that madness would readily provide.

Nearly everyone was convinced that the nonsense would end in tragedy; that's why many of my friends said, "Tonight there will be a wake in the rich people's house."

I remember how at five in the afternoon the majority of people had massed together on the slope of the mountain. There was one group that laid out an immense blanket in case Cesarín tumbled downhill, as was most likely. The only ones to climb up to the summit with him were his two closest friends, his stepbrothers, stepparents, and the priest. Clementina, despite the optimism she tried to express with her words of encouragement, found she was nervous. A wave of sorrow washed over her plump and ashen face, while doubt and wonder gushed forth from her tiny eyes. Don Juan José de Jesús Antonio de la Sierra just scratched his chin and, once in a while, ruffled his sparse grey hair, while twisting about like a fool; Cesarín's stepparents enjoyed immensely the sight that Cesarín presented, giving his trial flaps; the priest prayed without stopping, asking at each moment that God's will be done; my friend Andrés had submerged himself entirely in the waters of amazement and observed all the details with the precision of a surgeon. I, very certain that Cesarín would again be split apart like a fulminating buzzard shot in midair, thought of how much time he would need to recuperate and of the day when we would again be present at the final attempt. Everyone else was sure that he would die from this.

At five in the afternoon, as had been anticipated, Cesarín began his run some fifty meters back from the abyss. A favorable wind blew by with a yellow cloud of pollen. The afternoon was cloudless and fresh.

The sun appeared to be almost sinking into the highest mountains and, nearly one hundred meters below them, the cluster of people who had come to watch Cesarín make his final lunge maintained silence (which in this case didn't have to be sepulchral). In the first few steps he slipped violently and nearly fell, but he knew how to maintain his equilibrium. He sweated in such a way that it seemed as if a sudden rain had fallen on his face, and, determined, he looked forward. Not at the ground, but forward. Perhaps at some birds (I remember a flock of parakeets) at that moment crossing in front of him without his knowing it. There were scarcely fifteen steps remaining to the edge when he slipped violently again (less abruptly than the first time). His mother covered her face, the priest grunted, and his stepbrothers, who had just started to run in the opposite direction, turned sharply and were at the point of cutting short his path, but at his father's unexpected cry they stopped a few steps from Cesarín, who at that moment spread out his wings and hurled himself headlong into the air. Everyone was dumbstruck at the sight of a tender bird that, with each clumsy flap, rose in more intense and rhythmic flight.

Clementina had drawn close to the edge to see the fall. When she realized that everyone had their eyes turned skyward, she burst out crying crazily, "He did it, he did it. . . ."

That night, rather than a wake in the rich people's house, there was a carnival throughout the town, and everyone commented on the incredible success. Clementina, who couldn't get over her astonishment, repeated continually to everyone, "He did it, he did it. . . . And you said I was crazy because I believed in him. . . ."

A week later, Cesarín had not yet returned. Some people, the priest among them, maintained that he had been transformed into an angel and would already be knocking at St. Peter's door; the most incredulous, "surely he was to be found in some neighboring village entertaining the people or dead in some ravine." Azucena Martínez, for her part, said only, "Like I said, Cesarín was more sorcerer than saint."

The fact is that nearly a month after they looked all over the region for him, he couldn't be found. This served to confirm the priest's suspicions. By then, Clementina had begun to prepare some wings for herself (only using buzzard feathers, for lack of any herons) to go in search of Cesarín.

DEMOCRASH

Dante Liano

Translated by Tina Alvarez Robles

Day broke unbearably on Sunday. The night before I had told Marjorie (my girl friend) look tomorrow I'll come by early for you to get that thing over with. That thing being voting. And the next day—blue skies, sun, people, I told you so: Sunday—at eight sharp we were at La Industria Park and it looked like all the s.o.b.s from our districts had thought the same because there was half of Guatemala forming a line When I said to Marjorie wait for me here I'm just going to drop off my sister at her polling place and there I go like a hero to leave my sister at the end of a snaking line that twisted and turned so that everyone faced each other—boy, did they hate each other—the umteen hundreds in front and the ones bringing up the rear, well, I'll leave you here, I say to my sister, and zoom back to Marjorie and her cousin and look I say the line is shorter in another section come on, and, *you can't always get what you want*, they didn't believe me, so then I yank Marjorie out and jam her in the shortest line When I go back to bring her cousin (the truth is, in front of room 5, where we were supposed to vote, there's no longer a line but a mass that sucks people up) a second before taking off I see Marjorie disappear through the door right away I rush off after her cousin and we get in a small line they created for us, another ten arrive, they get to one side of us and discover another line and so suddenly we're in the tangle, the line dissolves and so too bad they push we push you push I grunt and sweat rivers my shins are trembling, I remember tragic stories where people die crushed by the load of idiots trampling over them Gentlemen open the door! The police have shut the iron door and in the vestibule of the room we are several hundred individuals stuck body to body you can feel the ribs AND EVERYTHING ELSE of the guy in front because of course there are hardly any women Marjorie's cousin nearly croaks and I tell her let's go back all right she says and we try to inch out and everyone around us laughs we can't move we look at each other (terrified?) now it's all fucked up I think chastely Sons of bitches open the door! some men bellow. Calm down please—some guy says from above the crowd heats up (ow) Come on show your face! Push! Break that piece of shit! they keep shoving from behind and I feel irrational terror while a real smartass behind me says "I'm suffocating" real softly—gentlemen please (it's the guy from the registrar of voters, from above), calm down, don't push—Don't push your mama, open the door! a guy in a suit cries out "what's your beef" someone asks him "I'm a delegate and I can't get in" he says and so everyone laughs another shove and the ones in the back keep it up and Marjorie's cousin is leaving forget the nightmares I wanted to catch up to her but nope I couldn't even move—we're going to lower the door—(they're going to leave us locked in the vestibule) I'm right beneath the door and if they close it they chop me in half so I raise my hand and resist it/the others behind me when they saw the door closing pushed super hard/and suddenly, all of a sudden wham I'm almost in the middle of the vestibule OPEN UP YOU SONS OF BITCHES they all shout respectfully, the peace officers (emphasis on piece) intelligently insist on keeping the door shut A LADY IS SUFFOCATING, OPEN UP YOU ASSES, but they don't, Marjorie's cousin disappears from sight—the man from the registrar of voters throws us a frantic look and vanishes A LADY IS DYING they keep yelling and from behind you hear ONE, TWO, THREEEEEEE! and all I feel is the tremendous shove THIS HAS GOT TO CHANGE someone says and nobody laughs MY SHOE (he got it back later, the jerk) OPEN UP GENTLEMEN THERE'S A WOMAN

DYING UP FRONT (it was Marjorie) what a trip I think if this is democracy holy shit while I really wish the door would fall and I watch like in a movie that the door is bending PUSH ASSHOLES it bends more it curves now it cracks

CRASH!

and everything dissolves, the wood wall on the side splinters and the steps that climb against it fall to the ground with the wall and everything else and I'm running into the hall before I fall and they trample me (where's Marjorie's cousin) desperately I race inside "uneducated savages, you don't even seem like people" an old lady screams at us as she sees the *crazed* mob push in and I spy Marjorie's cousin and I grab her out of the rush to rest a bit Are we all right? yes, in one piece, so it's off to vote like GOOD CITIZENS besides we couldn't get out of the room anyway. I got in line. I marked an angry X.

Later, another. The last one. The police were suggesting that to get out we should shove against the people trying to get in. Class act idiot, I thought. Then I remembered my sister. I went to room 7 where she was. The mess was worse there. The huge red door was warping from the pressing mass of people. Two policemen got to one side. They looked at each other and decided to do nothing. All they did was smile. People are nuts, I thought. The reporters took photos... serving the people of Costa Rica and covering the elections in Guatemala, one was mouthing into a microphone while the other filmed a video. That's sharp, I thought. You're a reporter? (he looked at me like "what a question, man") Yes, he said. What a mess, I tell him. The people need an iron hand, he answered, what's needed here is the MILITARY POLICE. What a reporter, I thought. I didn't find my sister. Before meeting up with Marjorie I went walking around and confirmed that my ribs and EVERYTHING hurt. After that, you know the rest.

THE CLEAN ASHTRAYS

Bessy Reyna

Translated by Bessy Reyna

"Your arm surrounded me, bringing me closer to you for the first time. Tenderly, our footsteps descended, slowly, heavily, on the narrow steps, while your coworkers stared curiously at us. Our hands broke their barriers in a useless search for one another. Today, the awaited encounter, like every day at this hour; like every hour of the days, too. . . ."

Slowly, you put down your pen on your small, black, disorderly desk. The typewriter showing its keys like the irregular teeth of an old woman. The paper clips forming a chain, and the note cards—on which you accumulated so many ideas—now resting unclaimed in their cardboard box. The papers are piled up, loud laughter thrown right at your face.

(Vivaldi again—why can't they leave that stereo in peace?)

You used to remain behind, looking at her after the rest of your friends had left the house, while she walked hurriedly, impatiently. With her sad smile and those long sweaters to which she surrendered her body, she was so special. Different. You could never find the name to classify her in your mental archive, the one you started building around her almost unknowingly.

That mania of yours for renaming everything. Why can't you leave things with their proper names?

Her parting words now reverberate in the darkness, crashing against the windowpanes in a futile attempt to escape. Her gestures, simple—like everything she pretended to be—simple and so mischievously complicated.

Your gaze rests on the cigarette butts scattered in ashtrays all over the room, while beer bottles, piled up in the shape of a pyramid, laugh at you. Your reflection in the semilit mirror surprises you.

You will try to dial her phone number, and the table will passively accept your short, insistent blows, while hating you inside.

You had promised not to call her, to abandon her just the way you found her: alone, empty, without anything to offer. The black object with its twisted wires and small holes—which resembles a shower head—becomes a strong presence in front of you. Shouting at you, with that particular, sharp, annoying sound. (Will you break your promise? Your fingers dissolve at the touch.)

You hang up before her voice starts to draw you in again, and her sensuality penetrates you, kissing your ear and your skin just as before.

As is by now her custom, she takes a cigarette from the pack you threw on the paper napkin. (Why do you always cover napkins with small, black, insecure lines?) She, fragile, lackadaisical, next to you, plays with your lighter, while you avidly, silently, absorb her face, anticipating the moment her lips will build that wall of smoke, which you will be unable to destroy.

Your attention returns to your desk. The objects greet you once again, and you become aware of the uselessness of trying to organize them or your life. You will go and find her. Try to explain, clear up the mess.

Once again, a rainy Sunday pulls you to her house. You don't care about uncovering your motives or trying to analyze why you want her so much on Sundays... Sundays?

The light from the lonely ashtray disrupts your intimacy. It's playing a game of colors with the rays filtering from the outside. You must work on your research. You must finish it, present it at the next conference.

Your books now occupy the small space that used to be empty in her room.

Her fingers caress you fleetingly, while she walks toward the stereo, and soon the room will be filled with the sounds of unwelcomed people. (You remember the color of her eyes; she can be such a child at times.)

You attempt to erase the traces of her small body impressed on your bed. Embracing her quietly, while her perfume surrounds you. You remember the number they give out to identify prisoners.

Will you leave everything behind, just like that? Is it so simple? After so many months of loving her, you are sure any misunderstanding can be cleared up. Your footsteps continue to offend the tiles in your room. You feel cold, just like that afternoon at the café, when you made love to her with your eyes, while the straws sank in the untouched glasses.

"For a change, I will have an espresso," she said seriously. The waiter, used to your presence there, just inquired with his eyes, holding the pad on that gigantic belly of his. "Cappuccino... as always." That day you felt fearful and cold. Attempting to laugh, in spite of the fear and the cold. Forcing a conversation, searching for the topics discussed so many times while sitting at that table.

(Our table is taken—what are those people doing there? If I could rent it, I would; that way it would remain there, always empty, just waiting for us.) The waiter's arrival interrupts your thoughts. That day you wanted to imprison her, keep her with you forever. Never mind the rain, the misunderstandings, the wall of smoke.

The clock chimes in once more, reminding you of your slavery. Flashing the vision of your life's daily routines. Books. Letters you go to pick up at your post office box. Research. Half-eaten breakfast. Lunch at the café. Clothes piling up, waiting to be washed. Crowded buses in which you ride, mostly standing, until you reach your office. Your coworkers discussing the probabilities of winning the lottery. The clock's sound continues in front of you.

Today you search for the memories scattered around your room. The small desk is neat, organized. A brand new typewriter on top of it. Clean ashtrays.

You notice the date, then suddenly realize that she died six months ago.

ORDERS

Fernando Gordillo

Translated by Barbara Paschke

The air slips through the bars awakening memories of fresh water and silk, the smell of sleep and silence glazes the first hours of night; as the door opens the sound of the chain is scarcely audible in the darkness while the prisoners seek their daily freedom in sleep.

The touch of shadows weighs down the stillness, the crouching guard tries to poke fun at sleep, caressing the curvature of his helmet and reminiscing about flesh; the prisoner starts to moan.

Gastric distress, gurgling at first, on the verge of moaning and crying out. Those nearby worry and whisper among themselves; suddenly, with the urgency of a crash, nausea, primitive and tumultuous, alerting the cell to vigilance.

Sleep escapes; rubbing their eyes, the last ones to wake up try to figure out what's happening. Through choking vomit, in trembling retching, the man expels leftovers until there's nothing left.

"This guy is sick!"

"Hold his head!"

"Give him a rag so he can clean himself up!"

"Keep his feet warm!"

"Put a wet rag on his head! He's sick, he's sick!"

Mournful spectators hear the violent murmur of the nausea calm down to give way to the "oooohs" that seem to come from the mouth of the stomach of the ashen man who is having convulsions on his hard wooden bunk. The "oooohs" become the howls of a wounded beast which spread throughout the prison, interrupting dreamers and frightening insomniacs.

With his hands on his stomach, the man goes through interminable choking which ends in convulsive gasps; now he's lying on his side with the circle of prisoners regarding him fearfully.

"Grab him, be careful he doesn't fall!"

"The beans didn't agree with him!"

"He's really a mess!"

"Tell the lieutenant!"

"He's throwing up nothing but bile!"

"Tell the lieutenant!"

The corporal comes close to the man, asks him something, reaches out to touch the sweating forehead and steps in the puddle of filth spreading out under the bunk. He can't avoid an expression of repulsion and disgust, think the prisoners; the corporal leaves the cell; a thick and foamy saliva slides from the man's lips.

"Here's the bottle of water!"

"What happened?"

"What did he say?"

"Don't bother him with nonsense!"

"What?"

"That's what the sergeant told me, that the lieutenant gave him orders not to bother him with nonsense!"

"But this guy is really sick!"

"How should I know, that's what the sergeant said! If they want more water let me know."

The corporal goes off, minutes pass, a bottle of warm water is put on the man's quivering stomach. Silently, the guard sees the moon come out. The beautiful summer moon! Among the prisoners old beliefs come to light, minutes pass, obscure rituals are carried out and nothing happens, minutes pass. Don't bother him with nonsense and this man's intestines are being ripped out in an impossible vomit; the gasping seems never-ending, minutes pass, trembling and palpitating, the groans penetrate walls and consciousness.

Compassion fills the prison, minutes pass, cries are beginning to call attention to the sick man, little by little the cries spread through all the cells: vicious thieves ruffians fences drunks innocent men rapists beggars scum sick men swindlers society's waste defeated residue, man, in spite of everything, man, against everything, man in an indignant and united cry of humanity.

"Silence!" The lieutenant enters shouting. "Silence, assholes! Silence!" Shocked, the corporal runs up to the lieutenant; the sergeant at his side nervously holds a machine gun, the cries cease, minutes pass. The corporal explains to the lieutenant what's going on; pistol in hand the latter makes his way to the sick man's cell, looks at him, asks him something, looks away from the filthy puddle spreading out under the bunk, keeps an eye on his gun, and leaves, telling off the sergeant for being such an imbecile that he can't tell the difference between a serious case and nonsense.... The beautiful summer moon deepens the night.

No one in the prison is sleeping; captives and captors are waiting for the lieutenant who's talking on the telephone. The groans that break and lacerate the air return, deep howls that seem to rise and just as suddenly fall to a whine. Minutes pass, again they put bottles full of warm water on the quivering stomach, everyone is waiting, the lieutenant is talking on the telephone.

"... Yes, ma'am, it's urgent.... No, he hasn't been shot.... Yes, ma'am, he's very sick... Wake him up, please.... Yes, I know, but really urg... Where can I find him? What number was that? Thank you very much, ma'am, excuse the hour.... Yes ma'am, first thing in the morning I'll send the prisoners to do the work.... Very well, ma'am...."

The wind lightly pushes the lantern hanging from a long wire, everyone is waiting, the lieutenant dials a number, a sound like a record at its end slowly runs the corridor until it reaches the last man: rrrrrrwww... rrrrrwwwwiw... rrrrrwww.

"Hello! Hello! .. Is the colonel there!... His wife told me he was there.... You don't know where he went?"

Pain isn't waiting, the man puts his fingers in his mouth trying to provoke vomit that never comes; to help him two prisoners lift him up from his stomach, minutes pass through the wall whitened by the moon, the time for the changing of the guard arrives, dogs bark, men come and go, no one sleeps, the lieutenant keeps telephoning, pain isn't waiting.

"Hello! Is the colonel there! . . . Call him. . . . Here, from the prison, sir. . . . It's because of something very important, sir. . . . It's because of a prisoner who is very sick, sir. . . . The doctor is out at his ranch. . . . No sir, it's not political."

Next to the desk three men wait impatiently, letters and signatures wait, the colonel's drink waits in front of his empty chair, the colonel makes signs to the men and continues talking.

"By whose order is . . . Go look for the judge, then. . . . No, I'm not getting myself mixed up in anything. . . . I said no, go look for the judge. . . . Whatever the judge says . . . No, call me tomorrow."

The early morning wind is coming up: cold and lonely. In the cells the prisoners who have surrendered to weariness sleep; a toilet flushes, minutes pass, sweating, freezing in every pore of his body the sick man clutches his empty stomach. The lieutenant and two aides go off in a jeep to find the judge.

"Sergeant! Call the firemen and tell them to send an ambulance! It'll save time, I'm coming right back with the order. Hurry!"

The jeep runs through deserted streets, shadows and dogs, stops, the knocks on the door penetrate the early morning. Minutes pass, a cart turns the corner in a faltering rhythm, the knocks get louder, hammering the silence, sounds are heard from inside, the light filters through the blinds. "Who is it?"

Wrapped in a blue bathrobe the judge listens, noting that the lieutenant has held on to his gun; his fat wife with rollers in her hair approaches, closing her pink flowered bathrobe. Minutes pass, the lieutenant talks, minutes pass. The ambulance siren slices the air; in the prison the sick man vomits again.

The ambulance's arrival livens up the prisoners, they make a little package of the sick man's clothing, they want to lift him up but he's having convulsive paroxysms and they leave him alone. A dry noise announces the opening of the ambulance doors, on his cot the prisoner curls up, violently trying to expel who knows what miseries that no longer exist in his stomach.

"Get a move on, he's inside!"

"Who is he?"

"It's cold this morning."

"It's a prisoner, hurry up."

"We have to wait for the lieutenant."

"Come on, let's go!"

The judge gets up, his wife follows, the lieutenant waits, outside the driver has turned off the engine and lights up a cigarette. The judge talks with his wife, it takes the lieutenant a half hour or more to convince him; the woman doesn't seem very convinced, the sound of conversation is heard in the other room, minutes keep passing. The judge opens a briefcase, takes out some stamps, his wife looks at him, he looks at her, minutes keep passing.

"You always let yourself get talked into everything! This can really get you into trouble! Who knows if it's really serious? If anything happens they'll blame you. It's already morning now. What'll it cost to wait a little bit longer? If anything happens you're going to be the scapegoat. Who would put up with enemies intriguing....!" The judge looks at her, she stops talking.

Rooster crows begin to open the day, the lieutenant leaves with the judge's order. What a night! The jeep moves and weariness comes over his eyelids. What a lot of coming and going! But there it is, no one's going to say the lieutenant let a prisoner die for the fun of it. Sure, the prisoners were yelling about it, it's the sergeant's fault, he can't tell the difference between nonsense and a serious case. What exhaustion! From the cathedral the bells toll, leaping over roofs, the jeep stops and the lieutenant gets down, showing the order.

The sergeant comes close, the beautiful summer moon is now gone, the sergeant comes closer, minutes pass and keep passing, the sergeant faces the lieutenant.

"Well, didn't the ambulance come?"

"Yes sir, it came."

"What? It left without the departure order?"

"No sir, the ambulance men left because they have orders not to carry corpses."

THE SHE-WOLF

Francisco Gavidia

Translated by Steve Hellman

Cacaotique,[1] now pronounced and written with total vulgarity as Cacahautique, is a village high in the mountains of El Salvador, facing Honduras. The brave general Don Gerardo Barrios was born there; later, as president of the Republic, he built a recreation ranch in Cacahautique, with four acres of rosebushes and four more of citrus, coffee slopes that yielded nine hundred sacks, and a house fit for the first lady, a woman of extreme beauty and elegance. A vast cement and stone patio, a pulp mill, and a trough to wash the coffee; a small stream that burbled day and night by the side of the house, all constructed on the hanging slope of a hill so high up that it dominated the plains, the valleys, and the rolling hills of coffee covered in blossoms; the nearby mountain where woodcutters with axes on their shoulders descended almost perpendicular roads; to one side, forests; to another, a sugar mill, at times processing cane, driven by oxen that moved in circles turning the mill, at times sheathed in a shroud of waste pulp, solitary and silent under a broad tree; further yet, magnificent peaks, one notched in the middle; bordering the farm, a ravine in whose abyss a torrent raged, hurling out drowned cries; cold air, splendid sky, and five or six pretty young women in town—these are the memories of my childhood.

My father bought the ranch from the president's widow and, leaving San Miguel, we lived on it for three years. I would have been about eight. I'd like to write more about that village, but there isn't time; however, I won't forget to mention one of the most magnificent spectacles that could be seen. From the small Plaza del Calvario a valley is visible that unfolds to the width of forty or fifty kilometers. In other times, forming forests of spikes, quivers on their shoulders, the innumerable armies of Lempira passed. In the bottom of the valley the river Lempa crawls like a silver lizard. One side of the river, as far as San Salvador, is called Tocorrostique; the other side to San Miguel is called Chaparrastique. Farther on from the valley extends the leaden green of the coastal forests; and farther, like the edge of a disk, the steel-blue curve of the Pacific. A tempestuous sky frequently wraps up the gigantic panorama in the passing clouds of a storm. Just as the valley extends to the sea, so from the sea hurricanes come howling for two hundred kilometers to lash at the trees in the mountains of Honduras. That's why you will hear that occasionally a traveler has passed the heights of Tongolón, where the two oceans are visible, only to be caught by ferocious winds and thrown from the horrible precipice.

Cacahuatique is a village that palpably represents the transition from an indigenous camp to a Christian community. The thatched roofs are interspersed with Arabian tile roofs that were adopted into colonial architecture without reservation. Hunters use shotguns and arrows. The vocabulary is a picturesque mix of Castilian and *lenca*,[2] and the creation myth mixes Catholicism with the terrifying pantheism of the local tribes. I still remember the dread I felt as a child when I passed by the hut where a woman lived, who, I was assured, turned herself by night *into a pig*.

This idea intrigued me at nightfall when I tried to get some sleep and saw the cornice of the bedroom wall, a churrigueresque cornice that mimicked the contortions of the snakes said to crawl around there late at night. I also thought I could hear steps that I was sure usually came from the next room and that some people attributed to the dead president.

Take away the village's Arabian tile roofs, the two churches, the innumerable mango trees imported from India and planted between 1840 and 1860; take away the cemetery crosses, the mayor's cotton coat embroidered with wool ribbons; the silk shawls of the barefoot villagers; abolish the horses and oxen, and now Cacahuatique is what it was before the conquest, with its idols nestled in the temple, whose sides offer an intricate mosaic of plants and animals and human figures, in the same way the human spirit is amalgamated with the beasts, trees, and rocks into the somber native philosophy.

Since you have now conceived the primitive face of this village, I begin my story, which is basically what was told to me by Damian, an estate manager.

Kol-ak-chiutl (snakeskin), whom the tribe called Kola for short, was a woman who openly went about getting rich, because she was a witch and a thief as well.

She had one daughter, Oxil-tla (pine flower), with brown eyes like the skin of a forest hare. Her feet were small; her hands, which had only tried winding cotton and weaving feathers, were as transparent in sunlight as tender leaves. Her breasts were like a ripple in the river. To complete her youthful beauty, her maternal grandfather had painted the prettiest birds on the child's cheeks. One day, Kola took her daughter to the country and there told her a secret. Three days later Kola went with her to the Arambala encampment where Oxtal (rattlesnake), the lord of the Arambala, dwelt with ten thousand bowmen, ever since he had seized the region by treachery. Invited to a party, he had left his people behind in the neighboring woods where they fell without warning upon the local tribe who were drunk on corn liquor. Kola and her daughter Oxil-tla put a cloth of woodmouse fur and crowns of quetzal feathers at his feet. Oxtal kissed them on the eyes and waited in silence. The mother made a sign to her daughter, who blushingly unfolded her shawl and put her idols made of river stone at the chief's feet.

Then Kola spoke in this manner:

"These are the four gods of my four grandparents, the fifth is mine, and the sixth is that of this dove who brings her family to breed with yours."

Oxil-tla lowered her eyes.

"Oxtal, lord of Arambala, has as many wives as a hand has fingers; each one brought a dowry worth one hundred canopies of quetzal feathers and one hundred bows of the type that the Cerquín archers use. Your dove cannot be my wife, but my attendant."

Kola rose, gently pushed her daughter from the door, and said:

"Your eyes are handsome like those of the sparrow hawk, and your soul is wise and subtle like a serpent: when the moon has come to illuminate the woods seven times, I will come back. Each child born to you of this dove will have as his spirit a silent viper or a jaguar with piercing claws. The young ones who go with me to the edge of the woods to call through me to their spirit, faithful friend for a lifetime, attract the strongest, most cautious, and longest-lived animals. Oxil-tla, walk ahead."

That's why, one afternoon, Kola had impatiently watched the tree in the patio where six lines had been made.

"Six times the moon has illuminated the woods," she said, "and still much remains to complete your dowry."

The vivid sadness of Oxil-tla was lit up for one moment by a ray of happiness.

Oxil-tla went in the afternoons to the nearby cornfields every time that the hum of a sling made the blackbirds of the region fly off, frightened; in such a way did the powerful slinger make his flint howl through the air!

In the green and flowering cornfield she had heard the song that she usually whispered between her teeth when she was in front of her mother:

Pine flower, remember the day
you went to the sun's rays
to offer this forehead which is mine
to the proud kiss
of the chief who guards the encampment?

Tell your mother, when the wide moon
has come for the seventh time
that I have to go to your hidden shadow
and that the stone of my slingshot
will make the warrior fall at my feet.

This singer in the cornfield is Iquexapil (water dog), the most famous singer known from Cerquín to Arambala; Oxil-tla loves Iquexapil and that's why she is delighted that her mother cannot collect a dowry of one hundred canopies and one hundred bows.

Kola, meanwhile, still ambitious for her lovely daughter to be the chief's wife, swears a sinister oath; with all her skill at calling up the spirits, she calls the devil Ofo to her side.

One night when a storm threatened, she went into the jungle and invoked the snakes with sunflower skin; the foxes that cry out in the withered leaves when a vision passes through the trees and sets their hair on end; the wolves whose stomachs are pricked by the spirit of the caves that makes them run to the plains; the creatures that sleep in ashes and the elves that steal the tribe's women to hang them by a strand of hair in an empty mine tunnel they have made home. The invocation touched the roots of the trees and made them tremble.

In the mist of the river, which had mingled its murmur with the odious incantation, Ofo, the devil of thieves, arrived and he spoke in such a way into the witch's ears that she returned content to her house, where she found Oxil-tla asleep.

Soon many thefts were noted in the tribe.

One man put a cloth of valuable feathers in the stone mill and hid to catch a glimpse of the thief.

He saw a she-wolf arrive, which he tried to scare off; the wolf leapt at him, devoured the man, and carried off the cloth. The people were terrified.

Kola, from the door of her house, waited impatiently for the moon to show its narrow disk from behind the mountains, like a stone dagger.

Now here's what happened one night. While Oxil-tla slept deeply, Kola got up, naked. The night cold is glacial, and the somber woman throws the heaviest logs on the cooking fire, in which enormous embers begin to revive. The witch then takes down the cooking pot of prayers, in which she will offer her gods the blood of hares sacrificed to bring on the rainy season. She positions this cooking pot in the center of the house, makes horrible leaps in the brilliance of the bonfire, offers sinister invocations to Ofo, and finally vomits into the prayer pot a leaden-colored vapor that remains there with the appearance of opaline liquid: it is her spirit. In that moment, the woman had transformed herself into a wolf. Then she went out to steal.

In the night silence, the clarity of the bonfire made Oxil-tla's eyes open. She looked around and called to her mother, who had disappeared.

Fearfully the young woman gets up. Everything is silent. She goes through the house and finds the pot, in which floats something both liquid and vapor.

"Mother," said the young woman, "Mother went to the temple and left the prayer pot dirty; a good daughter should not leave anything for tomorrow: I must get accustomed to regular work so that later on Iquexapil will see that I am a diligent woman."

Saying this, she bends down, takes the pot, and throws its contents into the fire: the flames flare suddenly, then continue to burn normally.

Oxil-tla puts away the pot, lies down again, and, to calm herself, tries to sleep and finally drops off.

Just before dawn, the she-wolf sniffs through the house, goes back and forth, whines, and looks in vain for her spirit. The day is about to break. Oxil-tla stretches and yawns gracefully. The she-wolf impatiently licks the spot where the pot sits. All is in vain! Before her daughter wakes, she reaches the door and flees to the woods, which deafen her howls. Although she returned on subsequent nights to howl at the door of the house, that woman remained a wolf forever.

Oxil-tla became the wife of Iquexapil.

The moral took these forms in the sad encampments.

---

1. Fertile region of cacao trees.
2. An indigenous dialect, more obscure than *pipil,* the common Indian tongue of El Salvador.

THE WOMAN IN THE MIDDLE

Arturo Arias

Translated by Sean Higgins

Slowly they descended, slowly they came to the cornfields. They passed from one side to the other, back and forth from one side of the shortcut to the other. They weren't stopping for anything. They went along cautiously, constantly shifting back and forth along the path so as not to feel the weight of the load that got heavier with each step. The load they carried on their shoulders, and the other one, the one that burned inside them as if they were breathing white-hot gas. The sight they had seen, following the patchy strip of shade that the trees projected over dry grass. The three of them, terrified beyond belief, each with a baby on her back. Feliciana felt as if she were crazy. She was barefoot, but as far as she was concerned, her feet had already ceased to exist. And her face was all swollen from not being able to cry, my God, from not being able to cry. She was almost running downhill.

Shots. Heard very close that time, as if they had come from the ravine, up through the cool trees. The foliage shuddered in the silence that followed. The wind stirred the smaller branches and leaves. Her heart was like a bloody bird that had fallen on the grass. Before she could even smell the gunpowder, she heard another round taking off like a gaggle of starlings. She passed her hand over her face to feel the concrete reality of her premature wrinkles. The clouds were suddenly dispersed in flight. The sun filled her, playing upon her senses.

She raised her hand a bit—an empty gesture, as Manuela was lost to her around the next bend in the path. She didn't hear, couldn't hear, Magdalena, who was lying in the deepest part of the gully that ran along the road leading away from the town. She felt as if she were moving within an aura. Eyes fearful, she searched for the river, visible at the southernmost end of the next turn in the path. She searched it out in order to feel that at least one thing still remained in its place. One single thing. And the river was still there—skeletal, silent, devoid of people—flowing through all this, forsaken by the heart of heaven.

The sun disappeared again. She chewed the dust, blown about by scarcely detectable breezes, that accumulated in her mouth and on the black branches of the pines. She looked up. The clouds loomed like gigantic black dogs, their fangs thirsting for meat, running along the horizon in search of boundless, unnameable prey. The dank, earthy wind felt like a dog's breath, and the fetid odor of death. The hunters were close by. She hurried her step; the colors and textures of her skirt stirred like those of a deep lake sighing restlessly. She felt the sweat running from her matted hair. But she didn't dry it. She left it to moisten her skin, as if its slow, salty flow could stem the escape of the scream that wounded her from within—Magdalena just lying there in the gully—but the scream that filled her would never end.

Her face was round. Her eyes, drawn and dried from so much sadness. Her nose, fleshy and wide. Her body had been heavy but had thinned as swiftly as they now descended the path, back and forth, with a load so unbearable it could no longer be felt. Over her red *huipil*, embroidered with yellow, green, purple, and orange, the sun, the heart of heaven, she carried a bundle to make the load more bearable. She squinted to look off in the distance. She hadn't heard another gunburst, but she noticed that the animals in the forest were fleeing quickly.

And in front of her, Manuela. She would appear, then disappear. Almost running out of pure fear. Behind her was only Rosenda. Only she, and no one else. But it felt as if the whole town were following her. As if they all were able to rise up out of the abyss and begin anew.

Magdalena lying there in the gully. Now everything was just memories. She touched her face again to be sure that she was alive. She was, but her memories were getting confused. Things seemed mixed up, fogged over. Grayness spread out over everything. The dry earth shifted beneath her feet. But now it communicated nothing to her. Now it was only dry earth; no corn grew. Her breathing was labored from such rapid walking; sweat ran over her entire body. Fear alone stayed with her.

Quicker. And not because of the load, but because she could no longer bear that feeling of breathing burning gas. The bloody bird had left her breathless. The shadows extended outward, black dogs waiting to spring. She felt spent and wrinkled, exhausted by the long walk. She would have liked to dry off the sweat, but her arms, weighted so heavily, could not move freely. She began to blink to get rid of the drops of sweat picking at her eyes like hungry vultures. Magdalena lying there. The shortcut provided only a narrow spot from which to observe the sky. Dry dust gathered in her mouth. She was within an aura. The river, almost dry. Faster. A lizard scurried fleetingly between her feet, losing itself behind a rock. She would have liked to linger awhile to look at it, but in that descent that had already become more like a fall, it was impossible. She felt the weight of her hands. Her whole body seemed numb, dead. She thought that she would never return, that she would have nothing to return for, and that she would have to stay in this abyss listening to her own heartbeat, just her own, for the rest of time. Faster, faster....

The skeletal river almost leaped in front of her. The next turn in the path was before her. She had to redistribute the weight to the left so her quick movement would not pull her to the right, causing her to fall into a dark chasm. She vaguely remembered her mother, who had taught her that skill. She wanted to remember. But the only thing that came to her mind at that moment was Magdalena. The whole town followed her, supple bodies tumbling downhill, nibbled at by the dogs, toward that black pit. It was always cloudy. Cold. Perhaps because of the bloody bird. That burning, incandescent gas. She was alive, covered with wrinkles. She chewed the dry, gray dust. Without corn. The turn in the path.

She rounded the bend and halted abruptly, but not quickly enough to stop herself from running up against Manuela's baby. The child let out a howl that seemed unending, like a siren. He swung his little hands in the air, joining them, separating them, joining, separating....

Manuela was stopped, frozen like a statue. As if she weren't alive, as if she were just another tree trunk. With her head erect, she contemplated an uncertain spot in the middle of the path just ahead, downhill. The taste of dust filled her mouth, asphyxiated her. The burning burden, the incandescent dogs. She wanted so much to be able to flee through the slit of shade cast by the trees over the dry grass. But her face was already too swollen, even for the heart of heaven. And the fangs wanting to tear that scream out of her. It would never stop. They had fallen into the pit. The hungry vultures would be picking at their eyes.

The men were coming up the same path. The line of heads was drawing near. They watched the women. Row upon row, row upon row. They approached with sure, measured steps. She had done so much walking, without arriving anywhere. And now she wouldn't arrive at all.

They seemed like wildcats by their movements and their markings; they lacked only fangs.

She felt a sharp blow on her back. Another sirenlike cry enveloped her immediately, like an aura. Once again the aura, but its intensity did not protect her. It was Rosenda, who had run up against her as she'd done to Manuela. Now the three of them were there together. Unable even to begin to retreat. She remembered the town, in ruins. She had existed once. Had existed. Now everything was in the past. The wildcats approached, row upon row of them. They were now facing the women.

Instinctively, she clung to a tree. Manuela and Rosenda did the same. If only she could dissolve into the foliage, evaporate like the water from the dried-up stream, extinguish the coals that burned her insatiably from within.

The soldiers took a few more steps toward the women, who held back a desire to scream into an immeasurable silence. The three of them looked at each other and looked once again at the rows of soldiers.

In fact, there was something Feliciana hadn't noticed. In the midst of the rows of soldiers walked three women. She first perceived their brilliant eyes and large mouths. She felt cold, and everything receded into shadow. It was impossible. It couldn't be. She felt an explosion in her ears, in her eyes. All of a sudden, shreds of memories fell about her, colored fragments that were lost in the recently desiccated land around her. She felt dirty, strained from the children's crying. She could barely take a breath, as if anticipating a more violent attack. Only the children protested. And the rows of soldiers drew closer until they were almost facing them. Now they were facing them. She didn't want to see.

But she couldn't help seeing, and she saw. The three women were approaching with their hands tied behind them. Two soldiers on either side, grasping them tightly by the arms. They were almost pushing the women, jostling them, dragging them. Their feet made strange patterns in the dust, leaving long lines that here and there branched off into monstrous apparitions disturbing to the eye. Then the fog.

The soldiers had almost formed a circle around the other women. That's why she hadn't seen them at first. Everything was moving, spinning around. Things began to fall out of proportion. And then she wanted to laugh out loud from having felt the silence of Magdalena lying there, in the deepest part of the gully that ran along the road leading away from town. Because she had seen the woman in the middle before. She tried to make it seem as though she didn't remember the woman's face, because the soldiers were watching her, watching her.... She didn't remember the woman's face. She was seeing her now for the first time, although she might have seen her once somewhere, in some market. Before, everything was possible. Before.

Because, yes, she remembered the woman's face, and it was not the first time she had seen it. The woman in the middle, that strange woman, surrounded by soldiers, with her hands tied behind her back, was her mother.

The long line continued to advance, uphill, until it disappeared around the turn in the path. Feliciana looked toward the place where the woman had disappeared, but she could see only the grayness of the underbrush.

JOHNTHE

Miguel Angel Asturias

Translated by Alberto Huerta

Laughter. A mouthful of teeth. They appeared ever whiter in his yellow face, covered as it was by liver spots, deposits of bile. Calamity, my Little God and Big God! The one with the poor was the Little God; the one from the city, with the rich, the Big God!

They say that he, Johnthedandy, was born from some robust male stock who, after a rainstorm of firewater, drunk and not knowing what he was doing, got involved with a silken young virgin whom he debased beyond words. But that was one of the many stories with which he whittled away the time when he drank firewater and had nothing else to do—just a little warmed-up water with the taste of fire.

Since his youth, he had liked the neighborhood by the sea, living near that immense, sonorous immensity, and there he built his shack, not far from a corner of high cliffs that squeezed the pools of still water.

With a shove of his feet—a mouthful of laughter sprayed from the sprinkler of his white teeth—he cast into the depths of that corner of still water the remains of an automobile he'd brought there with the help of an old, hairy, long-suffering mare.

Every day, morning and afternoon, the horse would drag those metallic shells, more like rusted iron than steel, which Johnthe extracted from a big pit near the piers of the old port; there the remains of unserviceable cars ended their days.

Did he plough? It seemed to Johnthe that he ploughed the sand, with the old nag dragging the frame like a rake across the beach or over the marshy roads. With neither shade nor company. Cactus. Toucans. Herons. And Johnthe, in his persistence, hurrying along the poor big beast that was hauling, step by step, the junk that he, Johnthedevil that he was, was casting into the depths of the sea. Without making a sound, the metal skeletons disappeared into that corner of tranquil water.

Laughter, white laughter in his yellow face, joined every old car cast into the sea, like a funeral. Did he seek to avenge something? He felt he did. Something and some people, by burying in the salty water cadavers of automobiles, oxidized, rusted, without windows or with broken or glazed windows, headlights without pupils, doors fallen like loose lapels, broken running boards, clocks without minute hands, seats with their guts disemboweled, axles like stumps of amputated quadrupeds.

Nobody in that town of coastal hovels asked Johnthedevil, Johnthedandy, why and for what reason he hauled these metallic shells of scratched and mutilated hoods from the old port to the sea. And they didn't ask him because they thought he was crazy. In any case, something strange in his head caused him willingly to make so much work for nothing. Besides, when someone doesn't have it all together, it's better to leave him alone, especially since Johnthe in his delirium didn't bother anybody. On the contrary, he was cleaning up that corner of the old port of all the metal that stank of urine and salt water.

"Oh, Johnthe," his wife stumbled upon him on one of his many trips, "it would be better if you'd cast the net over there; we have nothing to eat; your poor children!"

Without stopping, Johnthe took off his large, broad-brimmed straw hat, helped the horse along, scratched his head, and said nothing.

"Instead of exhausting that poor animal, you should fish for something. What do you get, I ask myself, what do you get, Johnthe, out of hauling those old wrecks?"

"Go home and tonight I'll explain it to you," answered Johnthe, as he applied the reins to the horse so it would move forward with the unhappy remains of an automobile which, in its time, must have been something magnificent and never before seen.

"Your children, Johnthe, are hungry."

"Let them put up with it. They'll eat soon enough. Right now I'm planting in order to reap later on."

The woman stared at him, unable to open her small, sloping eyes, cut like a jigger flea, fearful that indeed her husband might have lost his mind.

"Planting," she said to herself, distressed. "Planting what? Reap? Reap, unless.... It's pieces of automobiles he's casting into the sea."

The heat and the flies—the buzzing stuck on their sweaty faces; the buzzing was more annoying than the flies that never gave them room to sleep. Nor did the words that buzzed around them, as they rested on mats on the floor.

"Johnthe, you're very mysterious, that's what you are, and that's why you hide the little bit they're paying you to clean up the old port."

"No, Big Celeste, I'm doing it on my own. Move away from me, your body burns as if it were embers."

"That's not what you used to say to me when you were well-mannered, Johnthewell-mannered. In those days you caressed me and everything was all about getting closer to me."

"In those days, there were no children, there was no hunger. Children and hunger, Big Celeste, are the same thing."

"You're going to kill the horse and we're going to be left with nothing. Poor animal, it's not her fault."

"Poor me...." murmured Johnthe.

"To be honest, I feel sorrier for the beast, because it's not Christian and can barely haul that stuff that's no good anymore."

"Big Celeste, I know what I'm doing and why I'm doing it."

"My God, what industry! It suddenly seized you."

"It's not industry, woman, it's imagination."

"It must be a scheme. If by a better piece of luck you'd plough some little bit of land..."

The cars' submerged bodies appeared to float at the least movement of the water, but it was only an appearance. Buried in the marshy depths, they began to display beards, long fibers, very much like the dribble of ghosts. While swimming underwater, Johnthe opened and closed his eyes, blinded by the brightness of the sun, which multiplied itself in the form of round, golden coins, shaking among the fish, thousands and thousands of large and small fish that crisscrossed those structures, like a palace of cages, in every direction.

Dragging his feet, old Quiquirigato, who had the face of a rooster and the manners of a cat, came up with the following blessing:

"Johnthedandy, you must take these little nuisances of the tamarind tree, these silly little tamarind seedlings and these vegetable fingers from the *zingiberi,* and these powders from the bones of a frog, while your wife prays the Franciscan prayer of the Porciuncula. Because it seems to me that you're not altogether sane."

The secret palace of cages he possessed on the coast, covered with algae, shellfish, and strange dreamlike vegetation, where the light shone tacitly, sleeping, filtered, more crystalline than light, crystal of bluish water, kept Johnthe outside the world, lost in underwater visions.

"There's nothing of greater brightness, my dear Quiquirigato, than my Palace of Chacalis."

"Why of Chacalis?" asked the old man.

"Because when I swim through it the waves go *chacalis, chacalis.* That's why I call it my Palace of Chacalis."

"You only went and sank everything over there, so you could—" intervened his wife, Big Celeste.

"Only—" interrupted Johnthe.

"And—"

"And what?"

"And nothing...."

"You do it to bother me, because you don't understand. Nobody here understands. Another way of thinking. Jesus and Mary, everyone should be so lucky to have my shells, my fish, my pearls...."

And for a long time he ended up living like an eel, scaly with salt, hair the flavor of tears, and shy of anything that wasn't the music of the deep sea, more submerged than out of the water. For him, swimming was like sleeping with open eyes, without touching the bottom, crossing the rooms of his palace of cages where sponges with holes slept, weeping, blue turtles, phosphorescent gulf-weed, white coral, algae, snails, and—he plunged several times in order to be sure of what he saw—the first oysters.

His wife didn't understand when he told her, in a confidential tone, removing his mouth from a piece of watermelon he had devoured with big bites, sucking and licking:

"If you could only see, Big Celeste, how happy I am, already the oysters are showing up."

"What a story, Johnthe, what a story. There have always been plenty of big oysters around here."

"Big oysters, yes, the so-called 'donkey-shell,' the one that releases a black sauce. But the little oysters..."

"For lack of rocks, they say...."

"For lack of rocks, I say,... ha, ha, ha...." Johnthe burst into loud laughter, a mouthful of white teeth that contrasted with the laughter of the black watermelon seeds.

"With you one never knows. Everything's a big mystery, a plan. Remember when you got it into your head that people abroad were going to eat iguanas? We set out to raise iguanas, but finding out later they preferred frogs, we set out to raise frogs."

"But this time, by God, Big Celeste, we won't be poor any more. If you could only understand things not as they are but as they are not."

"What am I supposed to understand? Because of you I'm like a deformed creature: when my stomach isn't big, my rear is; when I don't have the package in front, I have it in back; and I feel sorry for my children who are growing like rats!"

Not even the tracks of the cars remained on the roads where they were dragged. Wind and sand. And that was his secret. Only he knew the spot where the water took on a green color, the color of a glass bottle, losing its transparency and becoming cloudy. Only he. Only he and his shadow.

"They eat each other, as it they weren't the same blue," Johnthe said to himself as he looked into the distance. "The sea swallows the sky and the sky swallows the sea on the horizon, which is neither sky nor sea, only thirst, thirst for midday, which is calcined, calcining, thirst for water that turns into fire, thirst for the beach in flames, for the sand in flames...."

Pelicans of lime, with slow wings of lime... trains of turtles, their inquisitive heads and little hands and feet with the movements of oars... batrachians like suffocated minerals with eyes... rivers that empty into the sea like fish that go... herons of rose-colored cotton....

But better inside than outside, underwater, as long as he could hold his breath. He emerged practically drowned with a vision of greenish shells, his knife between his teeth, quickly in his hand if he needed to take it out of his mouth to defend himself against the big fish, although this time it enabled him to tear out the first oysters from the automobile bodies that had been converted into large rocks.

Jellyfish with agitated filaments promenaded their tiny shadows through the mourning of clams tied with unbreakable silk to the metallic cavities. Circles of cold fire opened and closed in rings of solar gold in waves of quiet water. Walking polyps dragged themselves, like long flowing hair, tangled algae. Zebra fish. Red fish. Pearl-colored fish. His entire submarine world. He didn't have enough air. He got out of the water with oysters he sold in the port. The blond employees at the pier would grab them out of his hands, paying him to reserve them, so they wouldn't have to eat any more canned oysters.

Johnthe's mouth would get dry, just thinking that in one of these oysters he might find his pearl, the pearl of his dreams, an iridescent little body that, without looking, they might grind up with their gold teeth, those beasts with shirts and ties. And that's why, even though it was more work, he offered to open them, oyster by oyster, so that they could devour them with pleasure. Some would accept this, but others, pearl hunters without a doubt, preferred to do it themselves with the point of their knives.

Sometimes, when he came out of the sea very early in the morning, amidst the rosary of snails and pink shells, Johnthe would stop with his baskets of oysters, close his eyes, and pick one of those precious items by touch in order to open it, trusting to chance. His heart beat fast, very fast. He held his breath. The pearl?

It's said that every job is shady, but his was darkness itself, since he didn't know what he was seeing. Didn't know, nor could he guess.

The black man Tobias Chacalito followed every step with question upon question:

"Where do you get the oysters?"

"What do you mean, where? From the sea."

There was nothing to explain. Chacalito felt strange on his sleeping cobweb feet as he followed behind Johnthe. He would lose him on the mountain, amidst the dwarfish brush of the coast, but he would come into sight further on.

Tobias stood still. The night bathed him, a night without stars. Champing at the bit, his ears immense, his body shaking, he saw with his two eyes Johnthe enter the sea and become a white shark.

"Chacalito now knows where his neighbor gets the oysters," the black man told himself before running back to the port.

And his testimony ended the mystery of where Johnthe gathered the oysters. Everybody believed Tobias absolutely, because he read the

Bible in English and had jars for analyzing rust.

"The bad thing," Chacalito confided to Johnthe's wife, who already knew about the pearls and who, in her search to find those kernels, checked out her husband's jacket at night, "the trouble is that the oysters of a shark don't give pearls."

"Come on, old Tobias, nobody can begrudge a bit of luck."

"Except if he asked the shark. . . ."

"But how can he ask it if he can't speak shark language?"

The woman bristled; she was dark, but she lost her color and turned white.

"What do you mean, a white shark?" she said slowly, shaking from head to toe. She bit her tongue. She was about to tell Chacalito, in order to contradict him, about the car frames that Johnthe took from the old port to who knows where. "Go tell someone else that big lie, Chacalito. Sure, a white shark, the poor guy . . . and my children little white sharks. . . . Better for me to just laugh."

"Just remember that he is called Johnthedevil."

"No sir, his name is Johnthedandy."

"And now you're rich, with lots of money . . ." insinuated the black man.

"Rich, no, but we don't lack for anything."

"You can tell, you can tell, the house solidly built and the roof is sheet metal."

"Chacalito," Big Celeste drew near the black man, "you ought to make it your business to help us, giving us a hand so Johnthe can find not just one pearl, but many pearls in those oysters he goes out to sell."

"It's possible, it's possible, woman," answered Chacalito, widening his eyes, "if we knew where he goes into the water, because that's where he changes from a person into a shark. If you follow him and tell me where, it would be an easy business."

"Yes, because then, having pearls, we would have money, a basket of pearls."

"I agree, big and small."

"Well, I'm going to follow him."

"Then we agree, Big Celeste," Tobias took his leave, "and so you'll be really rich, big shots. One doesn't get rich just from wanting to, but from ambition. But he doesn't have ambition; well, how is he going to have any ambition if, like a white shark, he possesses all the treasures of the sea?"

Abundance enters through the eyes. And so does envy. To the big house Johnthe added a smaller one, where his children who were already going to school slept. The oldest daughter was very lively and the youngest boy very sick, with red eyes, a huge stomach, and legs as thin as spaghetti. Dressed in a crepe robe tied around the waist with a golden cord, Big Celeste took him to the doctor in the port. Her hair fashionably done, her earrings, rings, little bracelets, squeaky, high-heeled, bright patent leather shoes—all new. On receiving her, the doctor bowed and addressed her as "Madam," and he examined her sick duckling, who was a disgrace, with great care, calling him "a precious child."

Where did these people, who only a few years ago were nobodies, get so much money?

For a long time, the treasury police, dressed in civilian clothes, followed him. They presumed that he was making liquor clandestinely in some cave. But for all their sniffing around Johnthe and the world he moved in, and the strict control established regarding the sale of liquor to those of age and under age, they couldn't stick him with anything. He got his money from the oyster business.

Feet, eyes, and ears followed him, and that's why he built a big canoe, so he could go to his oyster beds by sea and not by land. And from there he returned, when the sun was barely rising, because he released the cables of his boat after midnight, in the brilliant and sparkling nights of luxury. If a tempest or rainstorm threatened, he returned home to his cot, where he slept in the nude amidst the breathing of his wife, the breathing of his children, and the breathing of the dogs, cats, and parrots.

Whether asleep or awake, it was the same. The Angel of Hope passed over him with its sword made of clouds, while the great Chic-Chan, the serpent with round, obsidian, desk-drawer eyes where he hid the pearls, went around placing them in the bivalved mouths of the oysters that opened and closed in order to call out: Johnthe! Johnthe! in a twangy voice originating down in the chords of the windpipe.

"We have to buy a cow, Johnthe," his wife said to him from the other cot. The roosters were crowing.

"A cow?"

"And it must be black."

"Black?"

"That's what the herbalist said, in order to save the little boy. If we don't do it, he'll die. And from what I can see, today you didn't go to your Palace of Chacalis."

"I came back from the beach. There was going to be a big rainstorm."

"But it didn't rain, I didn't feel—"

"It rained very far out at sea."

"And you, white shark, were you afraid?"

"I don't like to be called that."

"It becomes you."

"It becomes me.... I am Johnthedandy. I like my name. What do you think? I like my name." He became alert in the morning light and asked, raising his head, his arms stuck under a speckled blanket: "And those black candles?"

"I bought them on Chacalito's advice, in order to illumine this Holy Christ when you're out at sea."

"One thing for sure, I don't like that saint of yours. They made him with the ears too big."

"All the better. That's how I wanted it. With big ears he listens to my petitions, my supplications, my prayers. And he doesn't like you either. He knows that the other day you said he looked like a crucified bat with a donkey's ears. Even though I told him, so as to calm him: 'Holy Jesus, don't worry about it, he talks like a white shark.'"

"If you were smart you'd ask him to make the moon full; when there's a full moon, pearls will rain down on my oyster beds."

"Pearls fall from the moon?"

"From where else? When it's good and full, ready to break open, spurts of little white drops slip out...."

"No doubt it's sweat."

"No doubt, cold sweat."

"Death, Johnthe. The pearls have something to do with death. As for me, now that I think about it, I don't like them very much. They're for lovers and the dead; better you don't find them, Johnthedandy, because I can't be your girl friend and I don't want to be your deceased."

His eyes turned into sleep. He was navigating through giant waves. In the boat he carried the black cow and the sick little boy. He didn't have eyes; he was sleepy. His temples beat like the sea. They weren't temples; they were two pieces of the sea of thoughts. What happened afterward? No, before. For him now there was neither before or afterward. What happened, happened without before or after. His voyage was always in the present. His boat, his little son, the black cow—everything was in the present. Everything fixed, fixed and in motion. Rocking in the immensity of the milk of slumber. He didn't have eyes, only sleep. Two eyelashed cataracts of sleep. If he were asleep, he hesitated, with the rudder in his hands, he wouldn't be there. Wouldn't be there? Far away? But what was far, and what was near? Neither far nor near. And what importance did near and far have? For him, nothing. It was all the same. He was, and that was enough. Enough of what? To be. To live. To be that day, between the serpent's teeth, part of the dog star, of the light, of the linked necklaces of waves, of the double fire of the sun and the reflections, of the sacred down of the palm trees, of the water that dresses and undresses until it becomes algae like galloping black hair. Heaven with the feeling of high clouds. A higher and higher heaven. Why return to oneself? Why disembark?

And the voice of Big Celeste, young, playful, her loosely flowing hair smelling like the chestnuts near her house. Her breasts. Upon which he wept from happiness, when, because she was only his girl friend, she kept him deprived. Then the wedding, the consent, and the renunciation of their bodies, and now . . . the pearls . . . riches . . . . "Better you don't find them, Johnthe, because I can't be your girl friend and I don't want to be your deceased."

He emerged. He had dreamed. He was awake. They brought him the news. He barely had time to tie up the boat. With a sack full of oysters he ran to the house. It was too late. Big Celeste rested on her bed, covered with a white sheet from head to toe. Only the shape. This is the way they transport angels rented for altars—all wrapped up. He lifted the sheet to see her. She looked like she was asleep. Cursed be the dream, death's helper.

His little children came and went through the house, aimless, like parts of a whole that had been broken. He didn't know if it was a hunch. He dropped the load of oysters that he carried in his jute sack and began to open oyster after oyster, in order to do something, to pass the time that was beginning to separate him from Big Celeste, not as time, but as eternity. He broke his nails; he hurt his fingers. He didn't scream. He held it in his chest. But he couldn't; he couldn't contain the stream of tears. The pearl! The pearl . . . that he had sought for so long!

Without anyone seeing, he hid it between Big Celeste's breasts. A huge pearl, like a kernel of corn harvested on the moon. The roosters kept crowing at dawn.

THE SWEDE

Ernesto Cardenal

Translated by Sylvia Mullally Aguirre

I'm Swedish. I say this first off because my strange case and the truly incredible events that I will try to narrate are due to the peculiar fact that I am Swedish. As I was saying, I'm Swedish and my name is Erik Hjalmar Ossiannilsson. I came to this small Central American republic (where I still am) in 1897, still a young man, to look for a strange species of the *Iguanidae* family that I consider to be a direct descendant of the dinosaur. However, my trip took a turn for the worse when, having just crossed the border, I was taken prisoner. Why I was taken prisoner cannot be explained; I have concentrated my thoughts for years on trying to explain it to myself without any success, and I don't think there is anyone in the world who knows. At that time the country was going through a revolution, and my Nordic appearance may have raised suspicions, and I couldn't make myself understood to anyone because I didn't know the language. But obviously none of these causes by themselves are reason enough to be imprisoned. Anyway, as I've said, it's completely useless to try to explain it; I was simply taken prisoner.

Nothing came from my trying, in broken Spanish, to make them see that I was Swedish. My conviction that my country's representative would succeed in rescuing me faded with time, as I discovered that this representative could not understand me, because he didn't know Swedish and had never had the slightest relations with my country. Not only that, he was an old man of ninety who was sick and was frequently taken prisoner himself. In jail I met a great number of important figures from the republic who were also accustomed to being imprisoned regularly: ex-presidents, senators, military men, respectable ladies, bishops, and once the chief of police himself. The arrival of these people, generally in large groups, caused all kinds of havoc in the jail: visitors, messages, packages of food, bribes to the jailer, mutinies, and sometimes even escapes. Because of the constant stream of new prisoners, our situation—those of us who were already established as more or less permanent residents—was constantly changing. They'd switch me from an individual, relatively comfortable cell to a hall containing one hundred to two hundred other people, or they'd lock me up in a hole where one body could hardly fit. Worse yet, if there were too many prisoners and all of the cells were full, they'd move me to the torture chamber, which might be vacant because no one was being punished at the time. Anyhow, it's wrong for me to say *the* jail, because there were many and they often switched us from one to another. I think I must have toured almost all of them.

That's how I rubbed elbows with all of the most important people of the country, and how, little by little, I came to learn the language. For a long time I continued to assert that I was Swedish, now with complete clarity and correctness, until I finally stopped doing so, convinced that if it was absurd to me that they should imprison me for no reason, it would be equally absurd for them to free me just because I was Swedish.

I lived in these conditions for five years, having long since given up protesting about my citizenship and without hope that at the end of the president's term my situation would be resolved, because he was reelected. Suddenly, one morning, some government workers arrived, and to my surprise, asked if I were Swedish. As soon as I said yes, they had me bathe, shave, cut my hair (things they had never done before) and dress in nice clothes. At first I thought that relations with my country must have improved admirably, even though for some strange reason all those preparations, especially the nice clothes, also made me suspicious that they were going to kill me. My fear dissipated somewhat when I discovered that they were taking me before the president of the Republic. He was waiting for me and greeted me warmly, asking repeatedly "What had I done?" in the manner of someone who doesn't mean what he says. Then he asked me eagerly if I were Swedish, and since I responded positively, he added: "So you know Swedish?" Upon hearing my equally affirmative answer, he handed me a letter written in a woman's soft handwriting in the language of my country and asked me to translate it. (Sometime later I learned that when the letter arrived, the government had searched in vain throughout the country for someone to read it, until fortunately somebody remembered having heard a prisoner yell that he was Swedish). The letter was from a girl who called herself Selma Borjesson; she asked, as a favor, for some of those beautiful gold coins, which she had heard circulated here, and at the same time she expressed her admiration for the president of this exotic country, to whom she sent a picture of herself as a memento: a photograph of the most beautiful woman I had ever seen in my life.

As soon as the president heard my translation (the letter and, more than anything else, the picture of the girl caused him profound delight), he dictated an answer in broadly gallant terms, agreeing to send the coins, although he explained that this was expressly prohibited by law. I translated his thoughts into Swedish with utter loyalty, firmly convinced that this unforseen usefulness recently discovered in me would be worth not only my liberty but maybe even a small position or at least official support in my search for the *Iguanidae*. But as a precaution, I added a few brief words to the letter the president dictated to me, in which I summarized my situation, pleading with the admirable girl to intercede on my behalf.

I had little time to congratulate myself on what had happened, because the president had scarcely finished thanking me when, to my great surprise, I was whisked back to jail, my tailored suit removed, and I found myself back in my previous lamentable situation. From then on, however, every day was full of hope, and in a short time, another bath, a shave, and a return of the tailored suit announced the arrival of the hoped-for answer.

As I had already predicted, this second letter had a long paragraph about me, warmly asking for the release of her fellow countryman. But, much to my dismay, as I had also predicted, I couldn't let the president know because he'd think that I was making it up, or he'd discover that

I'd interspersed extra words in his letter and he might punish me with death for my boldness. So I had to skip the paragraph that called for my release, substituting some very flattering words insinuating love for the president. However, in the answer he dictated to me, I again interjected an even more complete account of the situation I was in, taking the opportunity at the same time to dispel the romantic idea she had of the president and to reveal what he really was.

From that time on, the girl began to write more frequently, showing an ever growing interest in my case, with the result that the shaves, baths, and donning of tailored suits grew more frequent (this never stopped being a little humiliating for me) at the same time as did my hopes for freedom.

She gained more trust in me through the letters that the president dictated to me. I should confess that during the tedious and unbearable intervals between each letter, the idea of my freedom, along with the thought of my beautiful potential liberator, obsessed me day and night. The two became confused in such a way that I didn't know if it were she or freedom that I desired the most (she was my freedom, as I told her so many times while the president was dictating to me). In other words, I was in love and had the infinite satisfaction of knowing that it was fully reciprocated. But, to my misfortune, the president was very much in love with the same woman, and, worse still, I was the cause and promoter of this love, having made him believe that the correspondence, upon which my life depended, was for him.

During my long and anguishing imprisonment, I'd entertain myself by preparing the next letter I would read to the president (which was invaluable, because he wouldn't allow me to read the letters to myself silently and then proceed with the translation, but demanded that I translate as I read; in addition, he made me read the letter three and sometimes four times in a row, either because he didn't trust me or because it made him happy) as well as the new reply I would give to my loved one, carefully shaping and polishing each sentence, making an effort to imbue it with all the poetry and traditional beauty of the Swedish language, and even making up short compositions in verse.

In order to prolong the letters even more, she'd ask the president to respond to innumerable questions about the history, customs, and political situation of the country, to which he acceded with great pleasure. That's how he began to dictate long epistles, usually concerning the government and problems of state. Over time he grew more trusting, and as he confided in his beloved, he would continually ask for her impressions and advice. It turned out that from a squalid cell, I held the destiny of the country in my hands, without anyone, not even the president himself, knowing it. Through opportune suggestions and remarks, I would allow the return of exiles, commute sentences, and free many of my fellow prisoners, without anyone being able to thank me.

On dictation days, one of my greatest pleasures was being able to gaze again at her picture, which the president took out for, as he put it, inspiration. I began to ask her to send more pictures, but, as might be expected, all of them ended up in the president's hands. My revenge came in the form of the many valuable gifts he sent her, which always went out in my name.

But a new anxiety was growing at the same time as my love: in that immense collection of letters deposited on the president's desk, the history of our romance was written in detail; letters in which he was now scarcely mentioned at all, and then usually to insult him. In each of those letters, in a manner of speaking, my death warrant was signed.

As one could see, the topic of my freedom—besides love—predominated in our correspondence. We planned all kinds of escapes and imagined all the stratagems possible. At first I refused to translate new letters, at least not until they freed me, but then they sentenced me to bread and water. This, coupled with the even greater torment of not being able to read more of her letters, which had become indispensable to me, broke my will. As a condition of giving in, I proposed that at least the shave, nice attire, and bath should be given to me on a regular basis and not only on letter days. This was humiliating as well as impractical, but not even this was granted.

Later on, my loved one proposed a visit to the president to arrange my release with him (a plan that had the advantage of the president's support; for some time he had emphatically insisted on such a trip), but I was strongly opposed to the idea, because it would mean losing her forever. I then proposed that another beautiful woman should come in her place and plead with the president for my freedom, but this time it was she who vetoed the plan on the grounds that, besides being very dangerous, it would be too difficult to find anyone to play the part. Another proposal of hers, which we were on the verge of putting into action, was to solicit a fervent protest on behalf of my government and even a break in relations; I made her see in time that such measures would not only mean the immediate suspension of our correspondence but an instant death penalty for me. I was more in favor of waiting until the then-lamentable relations with my country should improve. But as she pointed out, with good reason, how could we convince the Swedish government that it should improve relations just because one citizen was unjustly imprisoned? The wildest idea was one that occurred to a lawyer friend of hers, who offered to get me extradited by alleging that I was a criminal, failing to take into account that the president would undoubtedly send me to my death the moment he found out.

Meanwhile, a new worry arrived to add to the others and that was seeing how, day by day, I was growing more dangerous in the president's eyes because of the tremendous secret and all the other innumerable confidences of which I was the depository, with the consequent threat that this knowledge posed to my life. True, her love (which grew all the time) constituted my greatest security, because he wouldn't kill me as long as he needed my services. On the other hand, this security tormented me; because of my services it was more unlikely that he would let me go. Even my old hope that some fellow Swede should happen to pass through turned into a new fear because of the possibility that he would read one of the letters and discover my fraud.

My love and I were busy in the preparation of a new plan that might prove to be more effective when suddenly, the event that had caused me the most anguish and terror and that I had tried to avoid with all the strength of my soul happened: the president fell out of love. To my dismay, it wasn't a gradual process, but sudden, giving me no time to prepare myself. The letters that now arrived were simply thrown into the basket, and I was only called from time to time to read this or that letter, more out of curiosity than for any other reason. He would make me answer them in brief and hurried lines, trying to put an end to the affair. All the desperation and mortal anguish of my soul poured into those lines, and in the few letters from her that I still had the chance to read to the president, I added the most tender, profound, and passionate pleas of love ever uttered by a woman, but with such little success that at times he'd suspend the reading in midletter. To add insult to injury, the letters she'd write me were more like reproaches for taking so long to reply and, possessed by jealousy, she dared to doubt that I was still a prisoner, even insinuating that maybe I had never been a prisoner in my life. The last time, I wasn't even taken to the presidential palace in fancy clothes but stayed in my own cell; a guard dictated the final and definitive break-up, and I knew it was over with her, my freedom, everything. The last heartrending words to Selma Borjesson had been written.

They left some paper and a pen in my cell, just in case another letter arrived, I suppose. Whether the president hasn't sent me to my death because he's thankful or because he might need me in case another love writes him in Swedish, or simply because he's already forgotten me, I don't know. I don't even know if my love, Selma Borjesson, continued writing or if she, too, has forgotten. (Sometimes, owing to the habit I have developed here in prison of thinking the outlandish, I have conceived an absurdly terrible idea: maybe she never even existed and it was all planned by some enemy of the president).

More than four years have passed since then, and once again I've lost hope in the termination of the president's reign, because he's been reelected again. In light of this event, I have decided to take the pen and a few pieces of paper, which no longer have any purpose, and tell my story. I write in Swedish so the president won't understand it if it falls into his hands. In the remote possibility that one of my countrymen happens by chance to read these pages, I beg him to remember Erik Hjalmar Ossiannilsson, if I haven't died yet.

THE BARRICADE

David Escobar Galindo

Translated by Elizabeth Gamble Miller

In the darkness he fixed his half-opened eyes on the entrance to the first aid station.

Blood was flowing steadily from his mangled arm, weakening him, but he had another reason for not moving: he scarcely remembered the immediate past, before fifteen minutes ago; the rest was unknown. Not a name, or a place where he had been, or the reason for this ungodly wound. All he had was a broken body, a foggy mind, and a very live fear, horribly lucid, like the fear when danger is not over.

He was engulfed in mounting confusion: How had he gotten there? Why was he in front of a first aid station? Further: What was this unreasonable fear of going into a place that was probably his only chance for survival? His body felt light as a feather as he stood up, but he didn't take a step. A strange gathering abruptly appeared at the door to the station.

The men were all dressed in white, were tall and thin, and their faces glowed with a kind of phosphorescent light. First they laid something on the ground. Something they were carrying in their arms. Then they looked up, their movements synchronized, and held their heads in that position for a few seconds. They were saying something he couldn't hear; tiny whiffs of smoke came out of their lips and became a cloud that completely enveloped them.

He raised his hand to his face, wondering if that cloud was real or the product of his debilitated condition. His arm was hanging uselessly like a withered branch. He closed his eyes to breathe better, and when he opened them the cloud was gone. All the men had their heads bowed, and in their midst was a flame that could only be from a fire of great intensity, a white fire. Minutes later they dispersed. Perhaps the blackness of the night made the flame they left seem so bright.

He tried to move, but it was useless. His legs gave way and he lay on the ground the way he had before. The door to the station was open, but no one had passed by it for a long time.

The breeze came up, dispelling the suffocating heat and bringing with it a sweet fragrance. Then it stopped. There in the middle of the street the fire flamed up blue, an indescribable blue. Breathing was now more difficult, and his mangled arm weighed like iron, heavy as a weapon. The entrance was still deserted. The fire was going out, leaving a dark spot that spread out like liquid. The air was filling with smoke. A transparent smoke, white, grey, violet, black, black, black....

At dawn they found the lifeless body. The blood from the wounded arm was there on the pavement in diffused reflections.

"Victim of a crime."

"Or maybe an accident."

"I think someone threw him out here...."

"Abuse of authority."

"He comes by here every day...."

"Help carry him in, please."

"How awful! So close.... He almost got here."

"Yes. Almost."

DEAD WEIGHT

Mario Roberto Morales

Translated by Tina Alvarez Robles

"Matrimony emerged in ancient times as a punishment imposed on those couples who violated the endogamy taboo. Jailed in the home, the guilty suffered the mercilessness of absolute intimacy, while outside, their neighbors threw themselves into the irresponsible pleasure of free love."

—J. J. Arreola

Oh my God, it was too much, I swear. And yet I don't think I can ever forgive myself. At the same time, I wonder what I could have done? A woman has her pride and her own way of thinking. I couldn't just fold my arms and do nothing. My mother always warned me. But I loved him. I always loved him regardless of everything else. Deep down—I realize now—I believe he loved me too.

It was eight years—certainly no mere pittance. Eight long years of courting and at the end—nothing. His attitude was always the same. I did what I did because I began to despair. My mother and her terrible advice probably had a lot to do with it, too.

Gustavo was always like that. A drinker and a womanizer. He could never hide his addiction to skirts. He would stare at women insistently, without even being aware of my presence. It was like an uncontrollable urge within him. And the drinking, my God, that was the worst. Especially those early mornings when he'd arrive with mariachis or when he'd bang on the door just to delcare his love for me. I would stop seeing him for weeks at a time. A few times I found out about some of his flings with women both my mother and I knew. He could beg forgiveness as easily as he had the affairs. My mother began to despise him but, charmer that he was, he'd win her over again come her birthday or Christmas or Mother's Day. He had a zest for life, I can't deny that.

But I could no longer bear his evasions. It had been eight years. So one night in the midst of one of his drinking bouts, I broke up with him. Proud as he was, he didn't come around the house for six months. I decided then—out of spite and to make him jealous—to accept Alfredo's proposal. He had always had my mother's approval. We were co-workers at the office, and he showed me his affection even in the simplest everyday gesture. During the days when Gustavo would lose himself in friends and women, Alfredo did all he could to raise my spirits. He'd accompany me wherever I wanted to go.

I knew Gustavo found out about my engagement to Alfredo because his sister works at the same company I do. He phoned one day to say it was urgent that he talk to me. And I, believing that the jealousy was having the desired effect, stupidly told him we had nothing to talk about. So then he spit out his horrible threat—if I got married he was going to kill us both, Alfredo and me—and hung up. Like a frightened child, the first thing I did—which was the biggest mistake of my life—was to tell Alfredo. Very calmly he told me not to pay attention to the threats, that they were childish tantrums, and that, on the contrary, we should speed up the wedding date. At this point my behavior started to get peculiar. First I agreed with what he said and set the wedding date for two weeks from that night. My thoughts of Gustavo became distant and dreamlike but filled with panic. When the night before the wedding arrived, I was still in this mental miasma. Then the nightmare happened. I was trying on the wedding gown when, without warning, my sister burst into the room, spilling the news. Gustavo had been shot at close range in a bar. He had six bullet holes in his chest and was in the hospital in serious condition. He had muttered my name and address so I could be notified. Without a second thought I threw the wedding gown in a corner of the room and took a taxi to the hospital. I don't know why, but my mother did nothing to stop me. At the hospital the doctor informed me that Gustavo was in bad shape; the chance of a fatal outcome was great. I thought to myself, I'll stay here until he gets better.

At three in the morning they managed to drag me away from there. My sisters, cousins, and aunts had arrived, as well as some of Alfredo's relatives, who begged me almost in tears to return to the house so Alfredo wouldn't find out. They repeated incessantly that I was to be married that morning at nine. At the exact instant that I was rethinking my marriage plans, Gustavo's sisters and mother appeared in the hospital room. We stared at one another intensely and broke down crying together. I won't get married, I said to them. I love him and I won't get married.

They hugged me tenderly, resignedly. Finally, my family was able to yank me from the chair where I was waiting to hear about the miracle of my beloved's recovery. That morning at eight, while everyone was still beseeching me to be sensible, to think of the scandal, that the guests would now be arriving at the church, I received the notice. Gustavo had died an hour before.

On our honeymoon at the hotel, Alfredo and I spoke with a strange coldness. Suddenly he started putting our things in the dressers and closets. I went to the window and stared out at the street. After a bit I felt his hands on my shoulders. I want you, he whispered in my ear. Right now the coffin is being lowered into the grave, I thought. The wreaths and flowers must be falling on top of Gustavo (like Alfredo on top of me). His relatives open the casket to see him for the last time and they see my bouquet. What faces they must have made when my sister went to place it in his hands so that everyone would know I wanted to give him and only him my heart, so that he could take it with him to infinity. It must have been like the silence that descended on everyone when, instead of turning around and throwing my bridal bouquet so one of Alfredo's sisters could catch it, I gave it to my sister to take to the funeral. Alfredo understood my gesture and kissed my forehead. I can feel the shovelfuls of earth, the flowers on top of Gustavo like Alfredo on top of me, sticky, grasping, moving above me like a worm on the earth, among the flowers, heavy like the dirt falling on Gustavo, on me, on the flowers of the coffin, heavy. *You got your wish, Alfredo. But it's a wish that will cost you dearly: first, because I despise a man who wins a woman's love through patience—it's degrading—and second, because we all know that in this country anyone can have a person killed for twenty-five pesos and think nothing of it.*

Oh my Lord, with this weight of flowers and earth on me, knowing deep in my soul I will never forgive myself, I think, what could I have done? No, who could have told me that from one day to the next my love would leave (with my bridal bouquet in his hands) forever and I'd be married, on a honeymoon, and thinking so much nonsense, holy virgin, without being able to say that one day I am going to throw off this dead weight.

SETBACK

Horacio Castellanos Moya

Translated by Barbara Paschke

> My real Honduran-Salvadoran
> conflict was with a girl.
>
> —*Roque Dalton*

"Don't get hung up about it if it doesn't work," whispered Eloísa, her breathing still agitated and her legs open. Her words floated like soft comfort in the darkness scarcely broken by the lamp on the night-stand.

Juan Ramón, kneeling on the bed, his hands resting on the woman's hips, felt miserable, his pride crushed. He thought he should try again. Fleetingly, he ran through possible explanations. He looked at his flaccid member. He held his resigned body over hers.

"I wonder what happened to me," he said.

"It doesn't matter, these things happen."

"The strange thing is that I really want to."

"Relax," she advised, while she grazed the man's back with her fingertips; she lingered, amused herself with the little bump of a blackhead. "We've already done it once. You must be tired."

"It's not that. Everything was going along just fine. Who knows what happened," he said, sliding his moist lips over the woman's neck.

Eagerly, he thought about the warmth of that vagina he had just stirred up with his finger.

He rolled over to the edge of the bed. He took the glass of whiskey barely visible on the rug.

"What did you do with your drink?" he asked.

Eloísa turned to look toward the nightstand.

"It's over there," she said, reaching out her arm. But instead of taking the glass, she went for the tape recorder and turned over the cassette.

"I'd like to be able to blame something," murmured Juan Ramón. "Like last night I screwed too much or something like that."

The heavenly warbling of "Close to the Edge" began to burble from the tape recorder.

"You know, I think I pooped out because..."

"Don't obsess about it," interrupted Eloísa. "It's normal. Francisco told me all about the last time the same thing happened to him, with one of his students."

Juan Ramón, seated on the bed with his back against the wall, downed his whiskey.

"He really told you that?"

"Yeah. He said that when he got up to go to the bathroom, the whole thing just fell apart and after that there was no way."

"Some consolation," commented Juan Ramón. "So that's why it happened to me. Francisco's bad vibrations are here: I'm in his apartment, in his bed, with his wife...."

"Don't worry. It's never happened with me."

Eloísa reached for her glass. She drank what was left of the vodka. She thought that she still hadn't gotten as drunk as she would have liked, drunk enough to drown any possible guilt feelings.

"I'm going to get another drink," said Juan Ramón. "Do you want me to bring you one?"

"I'll go myself. I have to go to the bathroom really bad."

He watched her get up, eyeing her slender olive body, her delicate features. His gaze followed her while she went around the bed, elusive, until she disappeared through the doorway.

Juan Ramón grabbed his penis with both hands. He began to stroke it with pleasure. It didn't respond. Damn! he whistled between his teeth. Before the night was over, it had to work; if it didn't he'd look like a shit. Besides which, she, while they'd been screwing the first time, half an hour ago, hadn't come.

When Eloísa returned, a glass in each hand, he zeroed in on her pubis, on the dark line that joined it to a perfect navel. A soft stinging scratched her diaphragm. He took the glass. He thought this whole situation was a grotesque irony: now that he finally had the woman he had desired for the last few days, he was acting useless, victim of a sensation of spacing out that kept him from concentrating.

Eloísa lay down across the width of the bed, using Juan Ramón's thighs as a pillow.

"Does Francisco always recount his affairs to you?"

"Sometimes," replied Eloísa. "That guy is half crazy, you know. From the beginning he warned me that he wasn't going to sleep only with me, that I could look for someone to make it with if I wanted to, it didn't make any difference to him."

"I'd like to get to know him," said Juan Ramón, rolling over to put the glass on the rug. Immediately, he caressed Eloísa's short hair, and slipped his hand between her small breasts.

"In a little while, it'll be OK."

"Maybe."

"Once he talked about you," she added, "that you were getting to know me pretty well and everything. He was half jealous. He asked me if we had slept together...."

Juan Ramón hummed that part of the song in which the voice of Jon Anderson resembles a plaintive cherubim balancing himself on the edge of the abyss.

"I don't think he likes you," reflected Eloísa. "He doesn't like Salvadorans."

"Why not?"

"He says they're very thickheaded; that's why they are the way they are...." she added as she sat up to reach for a cigarette. "You're not cold?" she asked before getting under the covers. Juan Ramón followed her, immediately rubbing up against her body.

"He gets along well with Nicaraguans and Cubans, but he can't stand to even look at *guanacos*. He says that deep down every Salvadoran has a little Marcial inside...."

"Son of a bitch!" exclaimed Juan Ramón, repeating and savoring the phrase that seemed witty and lapidary to him.

"He says you're all very sectarian and moralistic, far-out mystics.... He'll give Nicas anything they want, but *guanacos,* nothing."

"And he screws well anyway?" asked Juan Ramón, abruptly. "I'm an idiot," he accused himself in a second. "You're going to tell me that at least he does it better than I do."

"You're going to..."

"The problem is that he doesn't really know us," he hurried to get back to the same thought. "We're not all like that. I won't deny that Marcial went to school, but if we were all like that, we'd really be in trouble. I'll agree that we're semi-extremist, and that we fluctuate between complete foolishness and dogma, but that image of revolutionary monks gives me a pain in the ass. It's an untrue generalization."

"The majority are like that," said Eloísa. "At least the majority of those I know. You're one of the few exceptions."

"What happens is that the flock of sheep abroad puts on affectations. It can't be like that inside the country. Political-military discipline is one thing and mysticism is another."

A kind of restlessness tingled in Juan Ramón's breast as he felt that slight body in his arms and entwined in his legs, that coccyx pressing against his lethargic penis.

"And what does he think of Hondurans?"

"Imagine," murmured Eloísa, "that we are like your illegitimate children, and that's why we're never going to have a revolution, because we spend all our time arguing about whether screwing is good or bad...."

He rubbed smoothly up against Eloísa. He had the feeling that any minute his penis would react.

"He's not completely wrong," she continued. "When I came to live with him, you should have seen the great scandal that broke out in the organization. That's why I left it, because I couldn't stand them anymore. So much hypocrisy. The same comrade who masturbated with my slipper in the bathtub later came to accuse me, without the least bit of shame, of being a liberal, just because I wanted to live with a Mexican. It's impossible, you know. The revolution abroad becomes corrupt. You have to accept it. You can't live mechanically."

He began to caress her clitoris, licking her ear, until he found her lips, that miniature mouth, like a little rabbit. He felt that now it was almost hard, that at the least erection he ought to introduce himself rapidly into that orifice that was seething, beginning to lubricate itself, and that once inside there would be no problem; on the contrary, he would advance on that fantastic road that now was cresting splendidly. She was panting, contorting herself. Juan Ramón took his hand out of her vagina and grabbed his penis, ready to glide it in, but it was still limp. He needed time, a few more seconds. She began to moan. He brought the head of his member close to the opening, kneading it desperately, with no response; instead, it seemed that with each stroke it became more watered down, like a piece of useless shit. He crumbled, turning to one side of the woman.

"It's no use," he said, "it won't work."

Eloísa kept silent, recuperating from her excitement.

"It's better if I just give up," he reflected. "If not I'm going to freak out more."

"I was more excited this time than the last," murmured Eloísa.

Juan Ramón told himself that he was a shit, no doubt about it, incapable of satisfying this woman who was surrendering herself completely to him. A kind of remorse affected his breathing. He made himself think about something else, to escape from this vicious circle that was beginning to lock him in.

"When's he coming back from Havana?" he asked, inaudible in the final attack of "Close to the Edge."

"What?"

"When is Francisco coming back?"

"Week after next," said Eloísa, trying to sit up to reach for her glass, "according to what he assured me the last time we talked on the telephone. It has to be confirmed tomorrow. But it costs an arm and a leg to communicate."

"And if he were to come in right now and find us here, how do you think he'd react?"

Eloísa drained her vodka. She looked at him out of the corner of her eye. She felt tired. She heard the twilight warbling of the piece. She thought she was sleepy.

"I don't know," she said.

ESTEFANÍA

Carmen Lyra

Translated by Sean Higgins

On the deserted, interminable beach that runs from Barra del Tortuguero to Barra del Colorado, we found the driftwood cross, once painted black, now almost completely faded. Along the arms was a name and perhaps the first letter of a surname, the rest of which was completely illegible: Estefanía R. Rojas maybe; perhaps Ramírez or Ramos.

We'd covered many miles without coming across anything to break the monotony of the landscape: sea and sky to the right, the sandy beach in front of us, and to the left the vegetation of cocoa plum, almond, and coconut trees. The afternoon fell within that immense solitude. And suddenly, that blackish cross stuck there in the sand, its arms extended out against the vast blue sky. The sea had carried it this far.

Estefanía R. . . .

What would the woman who bore this name have been like?

And a row of feminine silhouettes, like those one might encounter on the beaches or in the banana fields, began to parade thorugh my imagination: pallid figures, withered, scorched by the sun, fevers, and the sensuality of man, amoral and innocent like animals. There is one who stands out in this sorrowful frieze. Would she be the one called Estefanía? The name has been erased from memory. The face a dark triangle in the midst of a tumult of dark hair, her skin toughened, her teeth very white, her feet bare, strong, and vinelike, her arms elongated.

How would she have arrived at the banana fields from the highlands of Revantazón or Parismina? Her life had brought her wandering from Guanacaste. I believe that in Santa Cruz she first had a little boy, by the judge most recently appointed an honorable magistrate of the Court of Justice, when she had barely reached adolescence. And, of course, the esteemed gentleman would not remember such an insignificant occurrence later. She left her infant son at the first suitable home and began to drift. Then another, whose name she couldn't remember very well, left her pregnant, and she continued wandering, wandering. A little girl was born. She became like one of those branches that flows in a river's current. Life deposited her with all her belongings and a daughter on a banana plantation in the Atlantic region. And thus she continued, from farm to farm, man to man, today with one, tomorrow with another, even with a Chinese commissary owner and always with the baby girl clinging to her like fungus on a fallen branch.

On one occasion she got involved with a Honduran, and she accompanied him to a ranch where normally only single men were admitted. This girl was the only woman they'd seen there. The laborers got together one night and attacked the Honduran's house to take the woman away from him. They stabbed him and did with her as they wished. No one knows why they didn't just get rid of the little girl, who would have been about three years old at the time. On the ranch where I knew her as a cook, she was as faithful as a dog to the son of the owner. The young man was handsome and friendly—she would have died for him. He came to the ranch every month to check on how the farming was going; these visits made her as happy as an angel's visits from heaven would make a saint. For him she'd even put up with being kicked by the ranch foreman during his drunken binges, just as he'd kick his own daughter and his dog; and for him she'd see that not a nickel was misspent in the commissary, that not an egg was out of place, that not a stick of kindling was carried off. Meanwhile, in the city, the profits reaped at the ranch paid for the membership of both the owner and his son at the Union Club; made it possible for the Señora, with her corns and bunions, never to leave her automobile; and enabled their daughter to dress very chic and go to Europe or the United States every year, bringing back the finest outfits and underwear, which left her best friends envious.

She put in a few years there, but when she was stricken with malaria, no one did anything for her. She had to grab her daughter and her few belongings and leave for the San Juan de Dios Hospital. Who knows how she could have done it with the little girl... because I don't believe that in charitable institutions of that sort they'd admit her with everything and the little one too. And in the city, the young son of the ranch owner didn't even remember the poor, sick servant. As for the lady with the bunions and her distinguished daughter, they were unaware of the very existence of that poor woman who had taken great pains to see that the ranch didn't lose an egg or a nickel; whose efforts contributed humbly toward paying for that automobile, those foreign trips, and that fine, fine underwear for the daughter.

The last time I saw her was upon her return from the hospital, on one of those trains on the branch lines that leave from Siquirres, in a car full of black men laughing riotously, black women dressed in all colors, chattering with the soft voices of Nicaraguan parrots. And always the little girl clinging to her, already withered like an old person, and so serious that you began to wonder whether or not a smile had ever played upon her lips. It was really distressing to see this little girl, whose eyes were hard as stones and whose dry mouth led you to think of earth that has never felt rain. The mother was dressed in sky blue and her daughter in yellow—such brilliant fabrics. Why had they put on these showy outfits? Between the two of them, the sadness of their life together had acquired a painful absurdity.

Who would have thought that this woman had just turned twenty-five? She was so thin that she seemed to be sucking on her cheeks; on her bruised, discolored skin her sclerosis shone with a sinister yellowish tone; and on her cheeks, shoulder blades, and elbows the bones tore at her skin. When speaking, she made a grimace that uncovered her decaying gums where her illness had begun to uproot her beautiful, white teeth with the same indifference that one would pluck away the petals of a daisy.

Upon arriving at the terminal she descended painfully, supported by her daughter, and was confused by the crowd awaiting the train's arrival. From there she went to look for a space along with the other passengers on one of the open, mule-drawn platform carts, used primarily in fruit transport, which ran on rails, bisecting the nearby fields. Where was she going? She sat down with her little daughter amidst a pile of sacks and crates. You could see she was having difficulty breathing. It's not surprising that she was tubercular.

The driver cracked his whip and the mule took off at a trot, pulling the cart on rails behind it. At the end of the alley where the train ran trembled the living spot formed by the outfits of mother and daughter, who were going off again into the banana plantations.

From which humble cemetary of those villages along the line had a flooding river or the waves of the sea uprooted this humble cross?

Estefanía R....

One of so many women who have passed through the banana ranches.

Behind us the cross remained planted in the sand, its arms spread open toward the immensity of the sea upon which twilight was beginning to fall.

TAKING OVER THE STREET

Manlio Argueta

Translated by Barbara Paschke

When it's Saturday. When she sees me as if she didn't want to. When I notice her. When I see she's looking at me. When I riddle her with a smile of ah, my love, you don't love me like you used to. And the black moon blade of her eyes enters my eyes. When she tells me here it is and puts the bundle on the table I just got up from to greet her.

When people talk about the secluded house in the San Jacinto barrio, only those old men who get home at night tired from working from sunrise to sunset, from the morning star to the evening star. When people say: only that little creature who comes once a week. Genoveva speaks to no one. Sometimes not even to me.

"They send the young ones here," she says, taking out a couple of oranges and some medlars from Usulután.

When I tell her thanks, put them down over there. And I sit back down at the table while she goes to the back room, to the little patio, and the basin under the lemon tree. When she says to me,

"My brother sent me this," and hands me a pen of seven colors.

When I tell her: no need to make such a fuss, I don't need the rainbow; I don't tell her this last part, I just think it. Therefore, I am.

When the *compañero*, the brother, told me four weeks ago:

"In the meantime, you can stay with some great-uncles of mine, they never go into that house." Like brothers, we always called each other brothers. "Take this radio so you don't get bored."

When I tell him the important thing is to be with the *compañeros* again.

When Genoveva comes back from the patio or the basin under the lemon tree. When coming into the room she asks if she can't offer me something. When I tell her no thanks. Oh yes, hot water.

No problem, she says. And again her eyes unbolt dark windows, making me fall into the abyss of her eyes. She goes out to the kitchen. The spurting noise of the aluminum coffeepot. The damp coffeepot makes a crackling sound above the hum of the electric kitchen. Her footsteps accompanied by her shadow count the baked mud bricks. The floor's red bricks. The music of her Turkish dress material with little orange flowers, like bits of phosphorus burning in the vastness of a clear sky.

When she tells me I'm going now, in a low voice so no one can hear she's talking. I scarcely see her lips, I hear a children's tale on her lips.

When I tell myself I must be getting old.

When the great-uncles arrive at night. When they enter the house which is a tunnel of trapped odors. When they see the light in my room through the cracks in the old door. When I hear them whispering on the other side of the wall. When I turn off the lamp switch and right away I'm dreaming.

When I say to my *compañero*, my brother (it's the same thing) that now I'm getting bored. Last night he came to visit me. When he tells me, in that comforting tone that gets on my nerves, that in order to take over the street you have to wait for the right time. When I answer back "And how am I going to take over the street if I never even go out in the street?"

When another Saturday arrives.

When I don't remember ever having said a sentence to Genoveva, only monosyllables unite us: thanks, aha, good, uhum, greetings, goodbye. When today I discover her in her childlike expression, in her colored curls that belong to a certain age.

How old are you?

When she answers this year she'll be fourteen.

When I answer her question, well, thirty, more or less, but at this age one is never sure. Urge to screw.

Goodbye. Until next time. And she goes leaving a trail of yellowish gunpowder on the red brick floor.

That time I saw you for the first time I was fourteen, too, and who knows how old you were. You probably hadn't even been born. Those things are incomprehensible. And you passed by in front of my house.

When she brings me a pitcher of hot water and a little jar of instant coffee.

When she tells me: I'm going now. When I tell her get going before it gets too late. The two of us alone in the house.

When she closes the door. When she leaves. When I feel her footsteps reach the corner. When she crosses the street toward the bus stop, in front of the orphanage. When she gets on the bus and disappears. When I wake up. When they take her by the arms and violently put her in a patrol car. When I let out a cry. When the great-uncles get up and ask me what's the matter and I don't answer because I pretend I'm asleep. When she refuses and they drag her to the car. When they ask her where she's coming from. When they knock loudly on the front door. When I leave through the patio in the back by the basin under the lemon tree.

When the old men say we don't know anything, we don't know him. When Genoveva's eyes have closed behind a red cloud of blood. The great-uncles stand firm, thrown to the floor. When the police kick. When I think I've got to go. When I leap over the fence to the neighboring patio.

When I take over the street and confront a November wind that makes one shed all the salt water, all the victories, and all that backward-upside-down freedom.

THE CENTER FIELDER

Sergio Ramírez

Translated by David Volpendesta

The flashlight passed over the faces of the prisoners once, twice, then it came to rest on the cot where a man was sleeping on his back, his naked torso glistening with sweat.

"That's him, open up," said the guard, peering between the iron bars.

The rusted lock grated as it resisted the key that the jailer kept at the end of an electric cable circling his waist to hold up his pants. With the butts of their Garand rifles, the guards tapped the bedboards and the man sat up, a hand over his eyes because the light hurt.

"They're waiting for you upstairs."

Feeling around, he began to look for his shirt; he felt himself shivering from the cold even though it had been unbearably hot all night and the prisoners were sleeping either naked or in their underwear. There was only one vent, high up on the wall, and the air circulated just around the ceiling. He found his shirt and put his bare feet into a pair of laceless shoes.

"Hurry up," said the guard.

"Can't you see I'm coming?"

"Hey, I don't need any of your lip."

"Yeah, I'm aware of that."

"Good, because you're gonna be aware of a lot more."

The guard let him go first.

"Move it," he said, poking him in the ribs with his rifle barrel. The frigid metal made him sick.

They went out to the yard; at the end of it, next to a mud wall, the leaves of the almond trees shone in the moonlight. In the slaughterhouse on the other side of the wall, animals were butchered at midnight and the air carried the odor of blood and dung.

Ah, what a beautiful yard to play baseball on. They ought to choose up sides here among the prisoners, or among the prisoners and the guards when they're not working. The mud wall would be the fence, some three hundred fifty feet from home plate to center field. I'd have to field a towering shot at that distance by running toward the almond trees, and after catching the ball next to the wall, the infield would seem far away and the crowd's roar for the throw would seem dim and I'd see the runner rounding second when with one leap I'd grab a branch and with a jerk I'd climb up on it and get to another branch on a level with the wall bristling with broken glass, and carefully putting my hands up, I'd hoist up my whole body, getting to my feet, and dropping to the other side, even though I might get hurt, I'd fall in the dumpster where they throw garbage, bones, and junk, tin cans, broken chairs, newspapers, and dead animals, and afterwards I'd run, getting pricked by the thistles, I'd trip and fall into a current of sewer water but I'd get up and behind me, in dry deafening crackles, the Garands would be stampeding.

"Hey, you there. Where do you think you're going?"

"I'm going to take a leak."

"You're pissing from fear, you asshole."

The plaza was almost proportional: there were trees next to the portico of the church and I was patrolling center field with my glove. I was the only fielder who had a glove; the rest of the guys had to catch the ball with their bare hands. At six o'clock at night we kept on playing even though we could barely see who was at the plate; I didn't have any idea of where the ball was except by its sound or until it came falling into my hands like a dove.

"Here he is, captain," said the guard, poking his head through the entrance of the half-opened door. From inside the room came the humming of an air conditioner.

"Bring him inside and leave."

He heard the door being locked behind him and felt caged in the naked room, nothing there but the whitewashed walls, a small portrait in a gold frame, a calendar with big red and blue numbers, a small chair in the middle of the room and, at the far end, the captain's desk. The air conditioner had recently been fitted into the wall and the fresh plaster was still visible.

"What time did they arrest you?" said the captain without raising his head.

He was silent, confused, and he wished with all his heart that the question was for someone else, someone hidden under the desk.

"I'm talking to you, or are you deaf: what time did they arrest you?"

"I think it was a little after six," he said, so softly that he thought the captain hadn't heard him.

"Why do you think it was a little after six? Can't you give me the exact time?"

"I don't have a watch, sir, . . . but I'd just finished eathing, and I always eat at six."

My mother was calling to me from the sidewalk that dinner was ready. I'm coming, Mama, there's only one inning left, I replied. But honey, can't you see it's already dark, how can you keep on playing? Yeah, I'm coming, there's just one more inning, and in the church the violins and harmonium began playing and people were saying the rosary when the ball came into my hands for the last out and we'd won another game.

"What do you do?"

"I'm a shoemaker."

"Do you work in a factory?"

"No, I do repairs at home."

"But you were a baseball player, weren't you?"

"Yes, I was."

"They called you 'Snake' Parrales, didn't they?"

"Yes. That's what they called me. It was because of the way I twisted my arm when I threw to the plate."

"Were you with the team that went to Cuba?"

"Yes, twenty years ago. I was the center fielder."

"But they cut you from the team."

"When we got back."

"You were pretty famous with that throw of yours to the plate."

He was going to smile but the captain kept looking at him with an angry expression.

The best game was when I caught a fly right in front of the stands: with my back to the wall I put out my glove and I fell backwards into the bleachers with the ball in my glove and my tongue bleeding but we won the game and they carried me on their shoulders to my house, and my mother who was making tortillas put down the *masa;* filled with pride and sadness, she started bandaging me up and told me that even though I was stubborn as a mule, I was an athlete.

"Why did they cut you from the team?"

"Because I bungled a fly and we lost."

"In Cuba?"

"We were playing against a team from Aruba; when I bobbled the ball two runners came in and we lost."

"Several people got cut."

"Yes. We drank a lot. You can't do that and win ball games."

"Ah."

He wanted to ask permission to sit down because he felt weak in the knees, but he kept quiet and stood still as if the soles of his shoes were glued to the floor.

The captain began to write and continued for what seem like centuries. Then he raised his head and the man could see on his forehead a red crease from his kepi.

"Why did they bring you here?"

He just shrugged his shoulders and looked at the captain, disconcerted.

"Well, why?"

"No," he responded.

"No what?"

"No, I don't know why."

"Ah, you don't know why?"

"No."

"I have your record here." He brought out a folder. "I can read you some passages to familiarize you with your life story," he said, standing up.

Down below on the field he heard the smack of the ball in the catcher's glove. It seemed so far away that he was uncertain whether or not he was hearing it.

But when someone connected with a pitch, the dry crack of the bat exploded in his ear and all his senses were geared up as he waited for the ball. And if that slam is in the air flying toward my hands, I'm going to wait for it with love and patience as I dance below it with my hands in front of my chest making a nest for it to fall into.

"On Friday, July 28, at five in the afternoon, a green Willys jeep with a canvas top stopped in front of your house, and two men got out; one was dark, wore khaki pants and dark glasses; the other was fair, wearing blue pants and a straw hat. The one with the glasses was carrying a suitcase with a Pan American decal and the other one was carrying a strongbox. They entered your house and didn't leave until ten that night, without the suitcase or the strongbox."

"The one with the glasses," he said and was going to continue, but first had to swallow a glob of saliva, "it so happens that the one with the glasses was my son."

"I already know that."

He was silent and could feel his toes getting wet inside his shoes, as if he had just waded through a puddle.

"There was machine-gun ammunition in the suitcase they left with you, and the strongbox was full of explosives. Now, how long had it been since you'd seen your son?"

"A few months," he whispered.

"Speak up, I can't hear a thing."

"A few months. I don't know exactly, but it had been a few months. He disappeared one day from his job at the factory and we never saw him again."

"And you didn't worry about him?"

"Of course, he's my son. We asked about him and made investigations, but nothing turned up."

He felt his false teeth coming loose and adjusted them.

"But you knew he was going into the mountains?"

"Rumors were floating around."

"And when he showed up in the jeep, what did you think?"

"That he'd come back. But he only said hello and left in a matter of hours."

"And they had you watch their stuff."

"Yes, he was going to send for it."

"Ah."

From the folder the captain pulled out more papers, typed in purple. He made a few revisions and finally took a piece of paper and pushed it across the desk to him.

"It says here that for three months you were passing ammunition, small arms, explosives, and pamphlets, and that government enemies slept in your house."

He didn't say anything. He only pulled out a handkerchief and blew his nose. Under the lamp he felt thin and burned out, reduced to a skeleton.

"And you, you don't put anything together, do you?"

"Well, you know, kids . . ." he said.

"Those kids are sons-of-bitches like you."

He lowered his head and looked at his dirty shoes, at the loose tongues and the soles all caked in mud.

"How long has it been?"

"What?"

"Since you've seen your son?"

He looked at the captain's face and pulled out his handkerchief again.

"You know he's already been killed. Why are you asking me these questions?"

In the last inning of the game with Aruba the score was zip to zip. There were two down and the white ball came floating toward my hands. I waited for it, raised my arms, and we were going to meet each other forever when it hit the back of my hand. I tried to grab it but it bounced away and in the distance the runner was barreling toward the plate and everything was all over, oh Mama, I needed warm water on my wounds, because—you always knew it—I always had the courage to field anything, even if it meant losing my life.

"Sometimes one wants to be merciful, but it's impossible," said the captain, walking around the table. He put the folder in the drawer and went to turn off the air conditioner. The sudden silence inundated the room. He took a towel off a nail and put it around his neck.

"Sergeant," he called.

The sergeant came through the door and, after the prisoner was led away, faced the captain.

"What do I put in my report?" he asked.

"He was a baseball player, so make up some kind of nonsense; put down that he was playing with the other prisoners, that he was the center fielder. A towering drive sent him back to the wall and he took advantage of it by hoisting himself up on an almond tree and jumping over the wall, but as he was running away toward the slaughterhouse, we shot him."

THE BRIDGE

Fabián Dobles

Translated by Steve Hellman

"That bridge you see over there isn't just any bridge. It has a name. Yes sir, we put it there. Look at the plaque: it says the government built it, but that's not true. We pulled it together by sheer muscle. But above all, one man put it there, from bank to bank. That's why we call it the Paco Godínez."

My beast panted heavily when we stopped in the middle of the bridge to read the plaque, above us the jumble of rugged storm clouds, and below, the river, that morning more Bull than ever, but not yellow: rumbling chocolate.

It was October and it had rained steadily the night before. We nearly had to swim in mud, and a little further on we had to make a path through it.

When we dismounted I still didn't know that the house and its corral had belonged to Paco Godínez. A boy wearing a canvas hat and with a machete stuck in his belt passed by, urging on a cow followed by a dog. A woman smelling of kitchen smoke greeted my assistant with the unrestrained fervor of old friends, squeezed my hand, and asked us in.

"Yes, of course you can; leave your baggage and stay here, if my brother doesn't mind when he returns," she replied to our request. "There's a spare room; another engineer used it a few years back."

The rough wall of the little room held a portrait that stared back at us with small and penetrating eyes.

"Yes sir, that was Paco Godínez," my assistant said. "When I went to Limón in search of new horizons, he was like that, about sixty years old."

The following day, my assistant with the leveling rod and I with the theodolite started work on the topographic measuring for the roadway project. He knew his native ground well and as such was doubly useful to me.

One night, seated in the corridor of the house, he told me:

"There, a little higher than where the Paco Godínez is, was the cable ferry. He built it with the help of my dad and the others. I don't know how, but that man knew everything. He had a head and hands that were one. If others could castrate pigs and help a mare through a tough labor, Godínez could do it too, but he could also butcher to perfection or shoe horses like a pro. If my aunt Honoria was a storehouse of medicinal herbs and poultices, Godínez was not only better, but he went to Guápiles and returned with the prescription that truly cured. He caught a live *terciopelo*[1] like he was playing, only to show us himself how to take the venom out for snake salve, or he prepared an ointment for pigs and cattle that terrified them like the hand of the vampires. Yes sir. What others could do with carpentry, he could do better, and even more so with bricklaying and electricity; like that time he took an automobile generator and its battery and put it to work with waterpower and ignited four light bulbs. He bet he could do it, and he won. Yes, with everything. One day a priest came and said mass in the open air. Know who helped him? Who was it going to be? Godínez. And thanks to Godínez, my dad and the others, who now have their lands deeded, didn't lose them. He called meetings, wrote petitions, gathered signatures, went who knows how many times to Puerto Limón and San José to engage lawyers and judges; the district attorney took him prisoner two or three times; he didn't the last time because all of us surrounded him with shotguns, some willing to risk everything. They set fire to his house, which was then scarcely more than a hut. Thank God, he got his way. The banana company, which was selling the Sotillos all that land from here to over there, couldn't evict us; and later neither could the Sotillos, those same people who pushed so long and so hard against building the cable ferry. According to Paco Godínez, they were opposed to it because the cable ferry was going to spread the parasites even farther and for the moment they had sufficient land on their side of the Yellow Bull for their cacao plantations and timber operations, and they wanted the rest to remain over here, waiting for them in peace and quiet for the future. Yes sir, but as I told you already, that man Godínez interefered again like a devil in the middle of the road, as they say, and aside from the fact that an engineer obtained—I don't know from which ministry or maybe from the municipality of Limón—the cable and the pulleys, he inspired us all to work on the thing, and in one month the first crossing was made. I can't tell you how much it cost us to haul the gigantic cable with a mule train and more yet to stop and bury it here and more yet to pass to the other side there for the same purpose and the damned thing came at us from below and we stopped it again and it came at us again until in the end we could do it only with a cable rig that Godínez improvised. And so much misfortune. Yes, just right with that cable ferry. We crossed over on it on the outside like on a circus trapeze, because there wasn't any material to make a basket, and you had to sit on a pole laid across the cables and, as I said, haul yourself across using a piece of rope. From one side to the other, and vice versa. Until the time came that, because the river grew larger than a young bull, you had to pass hanging and hollering at that dizzying height fastened tight to the trapeze. Until, well, it was bound to happen, it killed Paco Godínez's own wife. The pole you sat on was cracked or fungus had started growing in it, and there from up high in the middle of it she fell into the river. And worse yet, with the youngest child. They went overland to see if they could find a doctor, because Paco Godínez thought it might be an intestinal blockage and if not, so that he might know what it was then.

"Good Lord, yes, what a blow it was to the man. Just as he really put himself into doing and enjoying, it was the same with suffering. How he cried and cried. But as soon as the strongest tempest slackened—months and months he remained mute and like a sulking horse—he blamed the Yellow Bull; that bandit had gotten even with him, as they say, for having tried to tame it.

"'As for that masterless bull, we here are braver bulls,' he said to us, when he wrenched the stake from his heart and rejoined us. 'The cable ferry doesn't work. Now we see its reckless folly. People drowned before. Now it throws us in and the river swallows us. We have to build a bridge according to the rules. A bridge like a hammock.'

"The oldest men looked at each other again, thinking he's crazy. One asked him how and with what in these remote parts?

"Another was heard to say, 'We don't even have anything to fall dead in.'

"'And considering what we could have instead, we'd be better off buying more pigs and some young bulls,' said my dad.

"But Paco Godínez, yes sir, stopped in the middle of them all and shouted:

"'You're not going to leave me alone this time. You're going to help me, men. We have to demonstrate to this river that we can put a bridle on it, and a packsack and the saddle belt to boot.'

"And it was then that, among all the youngest men, we really began to dream. Dream of a bridge, yes. With masonry bastions; with cables yea thick, and heavy planks beneath, secure enough to go swinging or dancing on. Then we wouldn't have to unload the sacks of corn and the banana bunches and the fattened pigs hanging like drums from that cable ferry. And the youngest of us went to Paco Godínez's house, to tell him to count on us, and he appeared to rise above us, demonically content.

"'Convince your fathers, kids. Tell them anything's possible if they want it.' And we convinced them. Paco Godínez's petitions went back for another round with signatures from everyone, groups departed to Limón, to San José, into the same hassles... 'to be humiliated like beggars by the officials'—the man laughed— 'on the condition that we have the bridge.' And two years later a herd of mares and mules arrived with thick cables and cases of bolts and matching nuts and sand and cement and some bricklayers along with their foreman, although the foreman in reality turned out to be Paco Godínez.

"There was a bridge built, yes sir, only narrow and somewhat lower, nearly touching the river, and in high water one year the pitfall became obvious, because the Bull dragged it under. The damned thing threw off the saddle.

"Then I went to Limón. I had a lot of brothers, and I wanted to learn something. But before that, I heard Paco Godínez swear like the devil that things couldn't stay that way. 'You're going to be yellower, from anger, when we put a real bridge over you, one you can't carry away, Bull of the devil,' he shouted, standing among the old men in front of the disjointed bastions while they had a few drinks.

"This is the bridge, the Paco Godínez. Years had passed and I don't know how many petitions and trips to the capital, and formations of progressive juntas and hopes and deceptions. Finally it was just too much to do and to give; Paco Godínez offered backing to a candidate he detested and promised him that all the families from this side of the river would vote for him if the government would rebuild the bridge or at least send sufficient materials so that they could put it in place. 'Yes neighbors'—they say he said—'now you see that I expose so many grey hairs to the point of making a gift of my conscience, but it's because we need it. No more Yellow Bull, no pack saddle. The river isn't to blame. It is what it is, that's all, but it doesn't know it. The damn thing does what it can, and makes good fools and good-looking dupes of us in exchange for who it has swallowed. But we won't make any progress if we don't bow down with an iron bridge.'

"And not that candidate, no sir, when he rose to the president he was going to be; he didn't see eye to eye with Paco Godínez and the others: another government, five years later, sent the materials and workers. Once again, young and old found the time and the energy to help, though an engineer now directed them in person."

"The same one," I interrupted, "who lodged in this room?"

"The very same," my assistant responded. "Paco Godínez had time to wall the room and arrange a bed. And the engineer didn't lose any time. While he directed the works, he also spawned a son here. He gave Paco Godínez a grandson. The only thing was, Paco didn't live to see it... because when the work was just finished, he crouched in the very middle of the bridge to lift a toolbox, and he fell clear to the level of the split planks that he himself had helped split with fist and maul. They lifted him up like a dead man, and although he fought for several days, there was no chance in heaven. He gave himself up. It's called an infarction, I believe.

"You read the plaque. They all came to affix it: the priest, the commander, the governor, and the transportation minister. On a Sunday they put out music and notices for these inaugural activities. But the entourage was met with surprise. My dad and another neighbor guarded the bridge on that side. They had closed it with two strands of barbed wire.

"'No one passes here,' they said.

"Had they gone crazy? The minister reddened; the priest was disconcerted. The commander stepped forward with his hand on the holster of his revolver, and then my dad and his friend raised their machetes.

"'One moment, sirs; listen to us, or you'll have to kill us,' they said again and signaled to the other bank.

"Scarcely visible were the men's hats and the women's heads and then a cedar coffin, wrought on the afternoon of the day before. The midday sun shone in the cuts left in the sides by the chisel.

"'The funeral passes first.'"

---

1. *Terciopelo:* the black velvet, Costa Rica's deadliest snake.

WHILE HE LAY SLEEPING

Enrique Jaramillo Levi

Translated by Leland H. Chambers

Carlos awakened with difficulty after an unusual effort which, for a terrifyingly long moment, made him fear, while still semiconscious, that he would never wake up. It had been a sensation of profound anguish, similar to what one goes through when struggling to have one more orgasm after many previous ones on a night of intense pleasure and wantonness. And now he was sweating in the darkness of his room. Warmth descended on him like a great, viscous cloak. He recalled the immense bird that had fallen on his bed, enveloped in flames that lit up the infinite extension of the heavens. He saw himself burning again, screaming, and suddenly he again felt the pain lacerating his flesh. When he finally succeeded in returning the anguish to the plane where it belonged, to the exact dimension of the dream, spurts of water were streaming down over him. He had run to the bathroom and was now under the shower.

His urine, an intense yellow, was now vacating his bladder in a long, interminable jet. His penis was losing its stiffness little by little, allowing him to draw nearer and nearer to the toilet bowl. There are people who have an erection when faced with the idea of death, he thought. Years before, he had had a lover who would arouse herself by associating the final moment of her life with the most intense sexual climax that could be felt. And afterwards, that very unusual woman used to say, there would come a dream, equally profound and delicious, without any sense of limitation because she might have to get up at a certain time to go to work.

Thinking that if she had been a man she would have spent most of her life with a hard-on, Carlos observed himself carefully in the mirror of the medicine cabinet. He was a little swollen around the eyes, his hair was jumbled and his beard thick. The bitter taste that felt doughy in his mouth bothered him, and taking a little water in the palm of his hand, he sucked it up, only to spit it out with disgust. He didn't wash his face because he still wanted to sleep. There was no reason for the nightmare to be repeated.

He can't sleep. He lights a cigarette. Strange how he doesn't worry about smoking now. Before, when he was eighteen and spent his time in training, the only thing that interested him was keeping himself in shape. Angelica, his first girl friend, used to come watch him in the afternoon working out in the garage. She was seventeen then and had magnificent breasts which, according to what she told him, were the envy of her friends.

Squatting beneath a bar with two hundred pounds on his shoulders after having done that odious leg exercise nine times, he is just about to rise once more when Angelica suddenly comes into the garage sporting a pair of very tight shorts. The surprise and his exhaustion combine, making his legs tremble and causing him to lose his balance. Sensing that he is going over forward, he lets go of the bar with a great effort. It bounces against his heel. The pain is horrible. Angelica, motionless in front of him, doesn't know whether to laugh or cry out in pity. Leaning on her a little later, he succeeds in getting as far as the house. Although his foot is a great shapeless mass and the pain brings tears to his eyes, he manages to hold back his moaning. "Women are a lot braver than men," his girl friend had told him some days before, and he had nearly died laughing. "I know it hurts you, Carlos. For heaven's sake, forget your bet and let yourself groan if you have to," the girl begs him time and time again, but Carlos only shakes his head.

On another occasion, he remembers while taking out a new cigarette, Angelica was watching him work his abdominals on the inclined bench. They had been going together only a few months then, and he had not dared to go too far with her. French kissing, as it used to be called, was their most daring activity. Standing next to his feet, which were on the raised part of the bench and tied down with a leather strap, Angelica was counting out loud. He raised and lowered his trunk with his hands clasped behind his neck, trying not to pay too much attention to her so as not to lose his concentration.

Now he's getting tired and he starts looking at her from below while rising more and more slowly each time. How beautiful her tits look from that angle, so tightly fit into her sweater. He can't go on with the exercise because his penis, erect beneath his bathing suit, has gotten the girl's attention and she, blushing furiously, has had to withdraw to one side of the garage.

He is close to her now and even more excited upon noticing how her breasts are rising and falling because of her nervousness. She tries not to look at him, she doesn't say a word. Then Carlos, without thinking about what he's doing, brusquely pulls open her sweater, revealing that part of her breasts not covered by the skimpy bra. As he separates them from the fabric with his avid hands, he feels the girl's slight trembling transmitted to his fingers.

He see her breasts for the first time, whiter and smaller than he had imagined, two beautiful pears without the peel. Grasping her firmly by the shoulders, not daring to look her in the eye, he pushes her down. When both are on their knees, he lowers his lips to one flustered breast and is pleasantly surprised to feel how firm her nipple is. He puts her cold hand inside his bathing suit and makes her close her fingers over his penis. Wondering which must be the most aroused, his sex or that small breast he is sucking so enthusiastically, he slips his hand down until he feels Angelica's moistness and begins to rub.

Looking at her, he sees that she is weeping silently. He withdraws his hand and makes her do the same. He helps her stand up and put her clothing in order. "See you tomorrow," Angelica says before leaving, just as Carlos is about to ask her pardon. Both are pale. "Okay," he responds. He watches her leave and afterwards goes back into the garage and closes the door from inside. Stretched out on the narrow bench, he brings to mind the photos of the most recent *Playboy* he keeps in a box next to his bed and he masturbates without rushing, substituting

Angelica's face for that of the model, until he reaches plenitude. Then he remains asleep on the bench, on the bed now, with his cigarette still lit.

An enormous bird, still far off, begins to descend once again upon the sleeping body. Enveloped in flames it penetrates the enclosure of the mind that is dreaming it. The heat becomes more intense the more swiftly that great burning mass comes down. Fire makes contact with flesh. It devours it in dreams and consumes the body stretched out on the bed. The room is burning, the whole house is burning, but Carlos cannot situate the real fire because he keeps thinking he's in that garage where he does his exercises every day. He has awakened there and interprets that strange dream as a simple foretaste of the passion he is going to reach in his future relationship with Angelica. He smiles, thinking that instead of a girl friend he will soon have a lover, a charming seventeen-year-old lover whom he will go on molding in accordance with his desires and caprices because everything gives way before fire: the house now, the room before that, he himself a second ago without his even managing to wake up.

ANITA, THE INSECT HUNTER

Roberto Castillo

Translated by Sylvia Mullally Aguirre

Anita was a model child until she got the notion to hunt for insects. She was the best student in her school, had good manners, knew how to do many fine and beautiful things, and made friends among society's best. Whenever anyone mentions these things from the past, it stirs up a feeling of resentment at home. Anita was so special that, after what she did, Papa's anger and problems are very understandable.

Mama told me once that we were very poor when Anita was born, which you can't take too literally because she always exaggerates a lot. But it's true that Anita had hardly any toys in her youth, although the old man devoted his life to giving her anything she fancied. At first they made great sacrifices, but our parents firmly believed that while Anita was growing up good things should come her way, so that when she was older she could have the world at her feet. These predictions came true, in fact, little by little. From the time they named her, Anita lived under a lucky star. Papa consulted the almanac, and it turned out that her saint was Saint Eulogy. My Aunt Eligia got furious when she found out the name they were going to give her. She said, "What an ignorant man! With all due respect to the saint, such names in these times rob people of opportunities in life. I even remained a spinster because of it." Finally, they agreed that Anita was fine: it was modern, it sounded pretty, and it was also very Catholic because it honored none other than the mother of the Virgin.

I'm not saying this because she was my sister, but Anita had the most beautiful eyes anyone had ever seen. Everyone said that her deep blue eyes, her blonde hair, and the innocent white of her skin could make her into one of those dolls that are seen only in magazines from the U.S.

My folks discussed whether to send her to Catholic school or to the neighborhood public school when she reached school age. They couldn't agree, but my mother won in the end because she said that Catholic school would give her complexes. She said to remember that we were still poor and those old ladies only wanted money for everything. With all the lessons on manners according to Carreño that she'd received, Anita would be the model child at the neighborhood school, and when she reached high-school age we'd be ready to send her to the nuns.

Anita was the best-behaved child at school. She was always clean and well bathed; she knew how to sit, how to speak, and also how to address her elders. She was very different from the rest of her schoolmates, who looked like bums. They'd arrive with sleep in their eyes and their bodies covered with dirt from not bathing. Anita represented the school in everything; she spoke at all the public events; at parties she recited and sang beautifuly: she was the number one student. Her more studious classmates soon began to call her Miss Stuck-Up, but the nickname didn't stick because the teachers were all on Anita's side. Even the director of her coed school would pick her up to go to classes and drop her off after school.

I'd been in school for three years when Papa quit his job as a lathe operator and began to work with APLAN, an agricultural machinery distributor. They put him in sales, where he made good connections because he knew how to speak English, thanks to the record course he'd taken. We moved, and Dad started making payments on the house we lived in. Little by little things got better: the old man started wearing a tie, he bought a secondhand record player, and we got a telephone.

He was so optimistic that, in spite of being a miser, for Christmas he gave Mama the collection of records, *Timeless Latin-American Music,* edited by none other than Reader's Digest. Anita changed schools. She transferred to the elementary school at the Central Girls School, which, although it was run by the government, had tradition and prestige. Things were getting better.

When Anita finished elementary school Dad had bought her a secondhand piano, and when the time came to start Catholic school she'd already taken enough lessons to be able to play. From the time Anita started high school, the old man became more grumpy, in spite of his optimism. He would say that those old ladies just cost money, that just because they'd spoiled her, the girl thought she was the most intelligent one around, and who did she think she was, Miss Universe? But Mama brought him to his senses by reminding him of Anita's great future.

While she continued her education with the nuns, the piano lessons were followed by private classes in English, swimming, cooking, interior decorating, and embroidery. During that time we had a car, an old Chevrolet that Dad bought in installments at a used-car lot. After that, Anita demanded that we join the UNICARD system, and later on Dad bought a membership at the swim club. He also became a member of the Casino, although this required pulling strings and using connections because they didn't want to accept him, even with money in hand. Dad got furious: "Who do those scarecrows think they are? The rich don't go to that place anymore; can't they see that it's in complete decline? Don't they realize that I don't want to go drinking with all those old fogies? Can't they see I'd be crazy to give those old farty and conceited ladies that hang around there the pleasure? Everything is just so that the girl can have a halfway decent place to go to have a soda or a dance once in a while. Everything is for the girl, not for me." During this time, Anita's friends were from the best classes. They never invited her to their parties. Sometimes Anita was with them at the casino parties, but never at private parties. Dad said it was better that way, that someone in the family could watch over her at the casino, but at those private parties you never knew... "There are always so many shameless and brazen rich boys at those parties. Besides, you have to take into account that, although they don't invite her to their parties, they always value Anita's intelligence and good education; that spoiled little Sara drops her off every day, and they study together very seriously, and she even invites her for an ice cream in the afternoons."

Around that time Anita began to fill her notebooks with dissected butterflies, which she stuck in between the pages. The first one I saw had beautiful shades of blue on its wings. Many schoolgirls did similar things, only instead of butterflies they collected leaves or flowers. But these same schoolmates became alarmed when they saw what Anita was doing. They started telling her that she was going too far and was getting dust from the butterfly wings on all of her notebook pages and books. When Mom found out, she told her to be careful; if the dust got into her eye, she would be one-eyed for the rest of her life.

For vacation that year Dad took Anita to Miami. She wore only American clothes; and even the stuck-up princesses were dying of jealousy, although they could buy anything they wanted. Dad said it was a good thing the girl looked the way she did so those wretched gringos wouldn't discriminate against her the way they do with people who look Indian.

After the trip, Dad got more serious about house expenses: "Don't waste so much because we have to spend months paying the travel agency for the tickets. We already had fun as God wills it, and now we have to work hard." But a few months later, the old man gave in to Anita again and took out some more credit. There was new furniture in the living and dining rooms, nice crockery, and the front of the house was fixed up by adding a couple of classical style columns.

Anita continued to be a brilliant student, and rumor had it that when she finished high school the nuns were going to send her to Paris. When Mama found out, she got all upset: "They say that women have a bad reputation in that place; how am I going to separate myself from my little girl; it's good that she's intelligent but they're not going to make her sick from studying too much."

My sister always stayed away from the neighborhood gang. Her stuck-up princess friends would laugh at her, saying, this or that guy is your boyfriend, Anita. They were extremely cruel to people. They used to call Pedro on the corner "Broken Butt"; he worked in a mechanic's shop and the monkey wrenches would tear his back pockets, and he would say "breaked" instead of "broken," because he hadn't finished elementary school. Poor Juan de Dios, who worked at the ice-cream parlor, also got pegged with ugly nicknames; they called him "Dog face" because of his elongated and decidedly canine features. Anita told the stuck-up little princesses that she had nothing to do with those boys, but they'd jab at her, "Oh! so it was with Broken Butt, eh?" Anita got so steamed up and furious that the stuck-up little princesses never teased her again, and they became respectful and considerate.

In the afternoons, from the school balconies, Anita, Susy, and Sara waved their hands at the boys who'd come to pay them a visit. They'd drive by quickly in their new cars or on big motorcycles where they couldn't get into the compound because a huge iron gate blocked their way. While speeding by deliriously, they could see little white hands, beyond the gate, delicately swaying like handkerchiefs. From the balconies they could be seen driving around, taking the curves at high speeds, shrouded in smoke and the sound of rubber violently streaking against the pavement.

Anita never dealt directly with these boys, only from the balcony behind the gate. At home it was clear that she shouldn't associate with them. Everyone knew that they took advantage of girls who didn't belong to high society. They'd take them for rides in their cars, and several of them would use one girl. Dad threw a fit when he found out one day that the girls who strolled down the boulevard on Sunday afternoons were called "prick-teasers" by those fast boys with a lot of money in their pockets. Anita was the type who went from home to school and from school to home, and those kinds of girls deserved what they got for geting into those cars.

But Anita kept wanting to mix with the high society. Dad told her not to rush things, to hang on a little longer. When you enter the university to study business administration, I'll buy you a new car; then you'll be able to mingle with the best and you won't have to ask anyone for a ride.

Around that time she began to sit motionless during classes. She'd stare as if in a void. When a mosquito flew by, she'd suddenly stretch out her hand, shut it violently, and trap it. That's how she collected a lot of insects. Sister Margarita would smile when she saw this, and she'd say to herself with parted lips, what an innocent creature of God. Nobody realized that a habit was born here that Anita would never renounce.

Later on her friends began to comment that while they were on picnics or enjoying themselves by gossiping about people on the porches of their houses, or when they were with their boyfriends at the beach, Anita would spend the time scrutinizing the bark on the trees in the patio of her house. When she had finished, she would reexamine it very closely. That's how she collected many insects. At first that's all there was to it, but then she started taking off her shoes to carry out this operation, and later on she wouldn't stop even when it rained.

She'd spend all Saturday afternoon looking for insects among the trees, and she liked to take a juicy bite from the bark of the almond trees when it had rained. In spite of this, no one got alarmed, because Anita continued to be the best student, always pretty and well behaved.

During this period, Papa's social status continued to rise. He now frequently arrived home late at night. He drank whiskey and played in big poker games. Mama was further upset because someone told her that the old man had taken a lover, and she was destroyed even more when an anonymous woman insulted her on the phone. None of this prevented Anita from being the center of attention. Papa mortgaged the house, and there were parties and trips for Anita's last year of high school.

She underwent the most drastic changes that year, but her intellectual output didn't falter. In fact, she displayed an extraordinary talent for mathematics and natural science, to the point that many serious thinkers believed Anita could become one of the best minds in the country. It's true that she became very quiet. Nobody paid attention, but she became too quiet. All the while her insect hunts became more intensive. When she caught them she was happy to pull them apart in a thousand different ways and scatter them in corners around the house.

Anita only hunted insects on Saturdays and Sundays, but once she finished her final exams she devoted all her time to them. She made a special net and was feverish in her activity. She began to hunt them at night as well. She would sneak out of her bedroom on the sly, late at night, and concentrate on the hunt. She ate less and less and became more pale. One morning she jumped the gate of our house. She was barefoot, and she swung the net violently and gracefully against the mosquitoes, butterflies, grasshoppers, beetles, golden beetles, and all the insects on earth. She went around looking for them and picking them up in the street, and then she rested in the dirt lot next to the mango trees. She bit the collected insects and then smeared them on her face, arms, and legs. Later in the afternoon, she came home with her clothes torn by thorns and fences; her face was dirty from smeared insects and she was trembling, but she exuded a strange sense of happiness. My parents were very upset: "What are people going to say and have you gone crazy, girl?" and Mom: "No, her brain was too weak from too much studying."

For quite a while she wasn't allowed to leave her room until she recovered, but she lifted up the floor covering and dug out tons of cockroaches. She tied them with threads, learned how to manipulate and the cockroaches obeyed her every wish. They'd walk toward the left or the right, according to the way Anita yanked the threads. She had a bunch of cockroaches tied together that submitted to all her desires. The folks spread insecticide in her bedroom and killed them, but she caressed the dead bodies and kicked, cried, and became hysterical. For a few days she remained that way, without leaving her room. She devoted her time to chasing spiders and to lifting up more floor tiles, but she didn't find any cockroaches.

One day she escaped from the house. It was the time she seemed more beautiful than ever. Two days later she came home at nighttime. She was covered with green grasshoppers, and on her face she had the sweetest and most sincere smile in the world. There were deep scratches all over her body from the thorny bushes she'd gotten into. She smiled constantly and sang pretty songs never before heard. When the old man beat her all over, she didn't even move a muscle. She withstood the beating as if it weren't meant for her; and the old man said: "This idiot is out smoking marijuana and that's going too far now; this is an honorable home and will continue to be one, and no one laughs at me like that."

They found a psychiatrist for Anita, who by now had graduated from high school. No one showed any enthusiasm for her graduation because everyone was worried about the things that were occurring. There was some happiness, but they tried to hide it; at home they thought if people concentrated on Anita too much, a rumor would go around that she was crazy. Nonetheless, the nuns gave her a special end-of-high-school gift. They gave her a dinner, they sent her off very warmly, and what a shame that this beautiful creature is bound for the cruel world.

According to the psychiatrist, she was cured by the next year. She couldn't enter the university because the folks said it wasn't advisable while she was undergoing treatment. Finally, the doctor said it wasn't very serious; she just had symptoms of a neurosis. Fortunately, they weren't very severe, and she had already managed to overcome them.

For some months we were very calm; Anita talked once again, she slept well and ate quite a bit. One day she escaped but returned in the afternoon, and the folks said, "Poor thing, she needed to get out and it wasn't serious because she hasn't returned with any insects." These outings continued, but things were calm at home until the day when rumors started to circulate that Anita was seeing strange friends in the parks.

One time she was gone all day and came home very late at night with her clothes torn. The old man became furious and couldn't control himself. He started to beat her, and Mom said: "Don't hit her, she's still sick, my poor little girl." The old man was crazed: "This thing can't be handled by psychiatrists, you have to give this donkey some good lickings so she'll learn once and for all that this is going to be her medicine."

After that she was strictly forbidden to go out. But after days of confinement and sadness, Anita convinced Mama to let her out into the patio. She thought she would die if she continued to be shut up, and she started crying. Mom said, my poor little beautiful girl, now you will be good; well, come out, but you behave for me. Anita no sooner set foot in the patio when she gave a push and with a single jump cleared the fence and ran down the street. Mama yelled hysterically, "Come back, Anita, don't be bad, I love you very much, that man will kill me when he returns because he'll say it was my fault." She kept yelling until she lost sight of her.

For four days she was gone, and it was impossible to find her even with help from the police. One Saturday morning she appeared, barefoot, wearing blue jeans that didn't belong to her because they were too big. She came in singing and didn't acknowledge anyone. Her face and hair were covered with mosquitoes. She was smeared all over with blood because she would smash them between her hands as if playing a game. The sweat, mixed in with the blood the animals had sucked from her, dripped down her face.

This time no one said anything. They didn't even hit her. They limited themselves to washing her and saying, "Look at what you're getting into, you're so ungrateful, after all we've done for you, what a disgrace for us, you don't even take into account that we still owe the psychiatrist money." Anita didn't respond, but just kept on singing and seemed as if she weren't in this world. Dad took to drinking for a week, and he was also acting like a madman. To avoid becoming the next troubled one, I was sent to live with Uncle Carlos and Aunt Lola until everything was back to normal.

Anita spent entire afternoons signing sad songs. She sat next to the fence she couldn't jump over now because she was watched too closely. The strange smile she returned with from her last flight didn't go away.

A few days later she started to vomit, and then they discovered she was pregnant. The old man couldn't restrain himself, and said, "This whore can go to hell, this was the last thing we needed and now she's really finished us off." The old man kicked her all over, and Mama had an attack of nerves that left her with an ugly lip twitch that still hasn't been cured.

Anita lost the child she was going to have. It seems that some girlfriends helped her for a while after she was kicked out of the house, but she also escaped from them. At that time I was very little, although I remember pretty well. Nonetheless, I found out about some things later on which I can't talk about because Anita isn't mentioned around here anymore. Ever since all that happened, Mama just spends her time stuck away in church and helps at charity meetings. The old man became embittered; he continues to drink, and his debts grow larger all the time.

Speaking of Anita, I only know that she became very sickly, she got typhoid fever, she's all emaciated and as a result is unrecognizable. They say that on the banks of the river that surrounds the city she searches for sandbugs and earthworms by poking her hands into the sand. She then gives them to the fishermen. For a time it seemed that the neighborhood gang was chasing and scaring her. When she started to run away, they would yell, "There goes the Bogey Woman." But all this was probably just a rumor.

Our house is so different now after the incidents with Anita; it's as if the memories don't even exist. The truth is, things are going well for me. The old man understands me pretty well, although he never jokes with me or confides in me. Lately he's gotten the idea that next year when I'm fifteen, I should go to military school.

MR. TAYLOR

Augusto Monterroso

Translated by Barbara Paschke

"Not so rare, though without a doubt a better example," he said, "is the story of Mr. Percy Taylor, headhunter of the Amazon jungle."

It's known that in 1937 he left Boston, Massachusetts, where he'd refined his spirit to such an extreme that he didn't have a cent. In 1944, he surfaced in South America for the first time, in the Amazon area, living among the natives of a tribe whose name I don't recall.

By the circles under his eyes and his famished appearance, he quickly came to be known as the "impoverished gringo," and even the schoolchildren pointed at him and threw stones whenever he passed by, his beard gleaming beneath the golden tropical sun. But this didn't disturb Mr. Taylor's humble nature because he had read in the first volume of the *Complete Works* of William G. Knight that if you feel no envy for the rich, poverty is no disgrace.

Within a few weeks, the natives got used to him and his odd clothes.

Besides, since he had blue eyes and a vague foreign accent, the president and the minister of foreign relations treated him with particular respect, fearful of provoking an international incident.

He was so poor and miserable that one day he went into the jungle to look for some grass or leaves to eat. He'd walked a few miles, not daring to look around, when by pure chance he glimpsed two indigenous eyes resolutely observing him through the underbrush. A big shudder ran up Mr. Taylor's sensitive spine. But Mr. Taylor, intrepid as he was, faced the danger and kept walking, whistling as if he hadn't seen a thing.

With a leap (that in no way could be called catlike), the native put himself in front of Mr. Taylor and exclaimed,

"Buy head? Money, money."

Despite the fact that the native's English couldn't have been worse, Mr. Taylor, feeling rather ill, did grasp that he was offering to sell him a man's head, curiously small, which he held in his hand.

It's hardly necessary to say that Mr. Taylor was in no condition to buy it, but because he pretended not to understand, the Indian felt terribly embarrassed that he couldn't speak English well, and he apologized and gave the head to Mr. Taylor as a gift.

With great joy, Mr. Taylor returned to his hut. That night, lying on his back on the precarious palm mat that served as his bed, interrupted only by the buzzing of excited flies fluttering about obscenely making love, Mr. Taylor, with great delight, contemplated his curious acquisition for quite some time. He got the greatest aesthetic pleasure from counting the hairs of the moustache and beard, one by one, and from looking right into the pair of almost ironic little eyes that seemed to smile at him.

Mr. Taylor, a man of vast culture, knew how to give himself up to contemplation, but this time he quickly got bored with his philosophical reflections and decided to send the head to an uncle of his, a Mr. Rolston, resident of New York, who ever since childhood had exhibited a strong inclination toward the cultural manifestations of Hispano-American peoples.

A few days later, Mr. Taylor's uncle asked him—a polite inquiry having first been made concerning the state of his health—if he could please oblige him with five more heads. Mr. Taylor agreed with pleasure to the whim of Mr. Rolston, and by return mail—no one knew exactly how—"I am very pleased to satisfy your wishes." Very grateful, Mr. Rolston solicited another ten. Mr. Taylor felt "extremely gratified to be able to be of service." But when a month later Mr. Rolston begged him to send twenty, Mr. Taylor, a bearded and coarse-looking man but one of refined artistic sensibility, got the feeling that his mother's brother was doing quite a good business with them.

Well, if you really want to know, that's the way it was. With total candor, Mr. Rolston explained everything in an inspired letter whose resolutely commercial terminology made the strings of Mr. Taylor's sensitive spirit vibrate like never before.

They immediately set up a company and Mr. Taylor agreed to secure and send shrunken heads on an industrial scale, while Mr. Rolston sold them at the best possible price in his own country.

In the first few days there were some bothersome difficulties with certain local types. But Mr. Taylor, who in Boston had received his best marks with an essay on Joseph Henry Silliman, proved himself to be quite a politician and secured from the authorities not only the necessary license for exportation but also an exclusive concession for ninety-nine years. It didn't take much to convince the executive warrior and the congressional medicine men that this patriotic step would enrich their community in a very short time and that later on all those thirsty natives would have the opportunity (every time they took a break from their head collecting) to drink a well-chilled soda, whose magic formula Mr. Taylor himself would provide.

When the members of Congress, after a brief but noble intellectual effort, recognized these advantages, they felt their love of country surge, and within three days they promulgated a law exhorting the people to accelerate the production of shrunken heads.

Some months later in Mr. Taylor's country, the heads achieved such popularity that everyone still remembers it. At first, they were a privilege of only the most wealthy; but democracy being democracy, in a matter of weeks, no one could deny it, even schoolteachers could get them.

A home without its corresponding head came to be regarded as nothing but a failure. Soon came the collectors, and with them, inconsistencies. To possess seventeen heads was considered bad taste, but to have eleven was refined. Collecting became so popular that the truly stylish were losing interest and would only acquire them as the exception, and then only if the head presented some peculiarity that saved it from being common. One very rare head with a Prussian moustache, which in life had belonged to a highly decorated general, was given to the Danfeller Institute which, in turn, donated, in the wink of an eye, three and a half million dollars to promote the development of this ever-so-exciting cultural manifestation of the Hispano-American peoples.

Meanwhile, the tribe had progressed to such a degree that it now had a promenade around the Legislative Palace. On Sundays and Independence Day, members of Congress passed along this cheerful walkway, clearing their throats, showing off their feathers, laughing, and looking very respectable, on the bicycles that the Company had given them.

Well, what do you expect? Good times don't last forever. When least expected, the first shortage of heads occurred.

Then the fun really began.

Simple deaths were no longer enough. The minister of public health was a sincere man and one gloomy night, when the light was out, after caressing his wife's breast for a little while, he confessed to her that he considered himself incapable of raising mortality to a level that would be agreeable to the interests of the Company, to which she responded by telling him not to worry, that soon he would see how everything was going to turn out fine and that it was better to just go to sleep.

To make up for this administrative deficiency, certain heroic measures were necessary, and the death penalty was established in a rigorous form.

Judges consulted with each other and elevated even the most minimal fault to the category of a crime, punishable by hanging or firing squad, depending on its gravity.

Even the simplest mistakes came to be criminal acts. Example: if, in a banal conversation, someone, through pure carelessness, said, "It's really hot," and someone else, thermometer in hand, could later prove that it wasn't really so hot, the former was charged a small fine and immediately executed, his head sent to the Company and, it's only fair to add, his body and extremities to his survivors.

The legislation concerning illness received immediate attention and was widely discussed in the Diplomatic Corps and in the ministries of friendly powers.

According to this remarkable piece of legislation, seriously ill people were given twenty-four hours to put their papers in order and die, but if during that time they were lucky and succeeded in infecting their families, they got as many more months to live as relatives they infected. Victims of milder illnesses and those simply indisposed earned the scorn of the entire country, and on the streets anyone might spit in their faces. For the first time in history, the importance of doctors who never cured anyone (there were several Nobel Prize candidates) was recognized. To fail became an example of the most exalted patriotism, not only at the national level but at the most glorious—the continental.

With the boost given to subsidiary industries (the manufacture of coffins, for example, flourished with the assistance of the Company), the country entered a period of, as they say, great economic boom. This growth was particularly noticeable with the appearance of a new flower-lined promenade where deputies' wives passed, enveloped in the melancholy of golden autumn afternoons, their pretty heads nodding, "Yes, yes, everything's fine," whenever some solicitous journalist smiled and greeted them as he took off his hat.

Offhand, I remember that one of those journalists, who on a certain occasion let out a wet sneeze he couldn't justify, was accused of extremism and sent before a firing squad. Only after his unselfish demise did the Academy of Language recognize that that journalist had one of the biggest heads in the country, but once shrunken, it turned out so well that you couldn't tell the difference.

And Mr. Taylor? By that time he had already been named Special Adviser to the Constitutional President. Now, as an example of what individual effort can achieve, he was able to make money hand over fist, but he didn't lose any sleep over it because he had read in the last volume of the *Complete Works* of William G. Knight that to be a millionaire is no disgrace as long as you don't neglect the poor.

I think this is the second time I've said that good times don't last forever.

Given the prosperity and success of the business, the moment arrived when out of the entire population no one was left except the authorities and their wives and the journalists and their wives. Without much effort, Mr. Taylor realized that the only possible remedy was to foment war against neighboring tribes. And why not? That's progress.

With the help of some small cannons, the first tribe was cleanly decapitated in three short months. Mr. Taylor savored the glory of extending his domain. Later came the second, then the third, the fourth, and the fifth. Progress spread with such speed that the hour arrived when—for all the effort the technicians exerted—it was impossible to find neighboring tribes to wage war against.

That was the beginning of the end.

The promenades began to languish. Only once in a while could you see some lady walking by, or some poet laureate with his book under his arm. Both walkways were once again overgrown with weeds, making the ladies' delicate steps both difficult and thorny. Along with heads, bicycles were also scarce, and almost everyone lost their bright optimistic manner.

The coffin maker was sadder and gloomier than ever. And everyone felt as if they'd just awakened from a pleasant dream, that marvelous dream in which you find a purse full of money and you put it under your pillow and keep on dreaming and the next day you wake up very early and look for it and find nothing there.

Nevertheless, the business was laboriously sustained. But already everyone had trouble sleeping for fear of waking up exported.

In Mr. Taylor's country, of course, the demand kept getting bigger and bigger. New inventions appeared every day, but in their hearts no one believed in them and everyone wanted little Hispano-American heads.

It was the final crisis. Mr. Rolston desperately ordered more and more heads. Despite the fact that the Company's stock suffered an abrupt fall, Mr. Rolston was convinced that his nephew would do something to get them out of this situation.

The shipments, which had previously arrived daily, shrank to once a month and included anything, heads of children, wives, deputies.

Suddenly, everything stopped.

One bitter, gray Friday, coming back from the Stock Exchange, still dazed by the shouting and the lamentable display of panic his friends had exhibited, Mr. Rolston had decided to jump out the window (instead of using a gun, whose noise would have scared him to death) when, on opening a package, he found the tiny head of Mr. Taylor, which smiled at him from far away, from the wild Amazon jungle, with the fake smile of a child who seems to be saying, "I'm sorry, I'm sorry, I won't do it again."